THE
UNQUIET
DEAD

THE UNQUIET DEAD

Bryce Wilson

NEW PULP PRESS

Published by New Pulp Press, LLC, 926 Truman Avenue, Key West, Florida 33040, USA.

For information contact:
Publisher@NewPulpPress.com

ISBN-13: 978-0692542996 (New Pulp Press)
ISBN-10: 069254299X

This book is dedicated to my parents,
Kerry Maloney and Bill Wilson,
as the first one should be.

They started a war/
That we can't win/
They keep erasing all the streets we grew up in/

- Arcade Fire

THE UNQUIET DEAD

The only sound in the newsroom was the echo of Scott Molina's keyboard. It was 3 a.m., two hours after the morning paper had gone to print and two hours before the cleaning crew was due to come in. Scott was using the brief ebb between the two tides of the day to get some work done.

Technically he shouldn't be here. It was against company policy; or, more accurately, against the policy of the conglomerate that had absorbed the company ten years ago. But the old boys' network still counted for something, if not as much as it once had, and Scott's habit of afterhours writing was indulged. He supposed it was only a matter of time until even this pleasure would be taken away from him, Russell couldn't have more than five years left in him as Editor-in-Chief before his cabin at Bass Lake and his grandchildren began to call to him in earnest.

The others who had worked at the paper as long as Russell and himself had either proven themselves to be affable men with no particular ambition or leadership skill, or alkies, burnt out even worse than he was. The uneasy fact was that the next editor would be someone who had no particular allegiance to Molina. How much longer Scott's own brand of shit, unobtrusive as it generally was, would be tolerated after Russell's departure was an open question. He would cross that bridge, as he had so many others, when he came to it.

Still, he would miss typing in the empty newsroom when the last of his privilege finally faded away. He had space to think here. He was fifty-five, his faced carved with heavy lines, offset by the pale, thick, horizontal scar across his left cheek. His eyes were underlined by heavy shadows. Still lean except for the slight paunch that alcohol had given him, with gray streaks in his short hair that matched the color of his steel-frame glasses. Scott had come up in a time when there were still typewriters in the office. He still did his best work to the rhythmic pounding of fingers on keys that struck back.

But even an editor as indulgent as Russell couldn't be expected to allow Scott to do his work on such an anachronism, so the only way Scott could experience the sensation was by pounding his keyboard as hard as humanly possible, with such force that he wore through at least one every six months. It wasn't the same, but it was better than nothing. The effect could only be appreciated if it was practiced in a quiet space, which The Telegraph only qualified as during this two-hour respite when he could be alone.

The sound of heavy footfalls on the carpet told Scott that he wasn't as alone as he'd thought. He finished the last sentence in his paragraph, a community calendar article he could have written asleep or under heavy sedation, before turning with a squint into the gloom of the bullpen, hoping he wasn't in for a problem.

He saw Sunny Wan approaching, with an ingratiating smile that could only mean that he wanted to bum a cigarette. Wan was one of the new breed of non-smoking journalists, though he would lapse at least once a month into the role of a smoking journalist. Scott couldn't quite bring himself to trust him; then again he couldn't quite bring himself to trust any non-smoking journalist. Sunny was Asian, though Scott was unsure of which ethnicity; he had a feeling, though he couldn't articulate why, that it wouldn't be OK to ask. Stocky but handsome, still a few years shy of thirty, Sunny had started as the big would-be breakout star. He had been recruited by the Telegraph straight out of college. From day one, the bigger markets had been sniffing around Sunny – Sacramento, San Francisco, even Los Angeles.

Scott could see why; Sunny had the makings of a good newsman. His prose was clean and his copy timely; he could write straight objective and op-ed with equal ease. He also had an accurate nose for bullshit, and the instinct to know just what issues to press and just how hard to press them to give real weight to what he wrote without actually pissing anyone off. He was humble without being falsely effacing, got along with management without earning a reputation as a brown noser. But there was something about Sunny that Scott just didn't quite like. The way he had handled the attention, maybe; it would have almost been better if he had been cocky or preened. His "aw shucks" manner struck Scott as somewhat disingenuous. It wasn't enough for Sunny to receive the attention – he had to be loved as a super nice guy as well. You had to be careful of guys who wanted to have their cake and eat it too. You never knew which option they would choose if their hands were forced.

What he had never had was that breakout piece that would give him the momentum to make him irresistible to the big boys at the larger markets. Though smart, he was too amiable to be aggressive. The big markets needed their reporters to be attack dogs, to dig up dirt, not simply notice when someone tracked it through the living room. Sunny wasn't an attack dog; with his affable smile and trademark Hawaiian shirts he was closer to a big friendly Labrador. They waited and waited for Sunny to bring them something more than an easily retrieved dead duck. He never did. Unless something big happened soon, Sunny Wan would spend the rest of his career on The Telegraph, or a paper awfully similar. Just another talented player who never had the right stuff to be called off of the farm team and into the majors.

"Hey Scott, I hate to ask," Sunny began, but before he could finish Scott had already grabbed the yellow pack of American Spirits off his desktop and shrugged on his pea coat.

"Come on," he said. "I was just about to have one anyway."

They strode through the cavernous hall space, the buzz of the overhead fluorescents the only sound now that Scott's typing had ceased.

"What are you doing here so late?" Scott asked. Sunny shrugged, "Just had a little copy to finish."

Though he wasn't sure of Sunny, Scott had to admit that he was hurting for company on his smoke breaks, one of the few times he preferred to be social. The number of smokers had steadily dwindled at The Telegraph, and he could use the company. Even if it was the company of someone he didn't particularly like. He buttoned up his coat as he headed for the door, and shook loose two cigarettes in anticipation.

They went to the front of the building. Normally, smoking was relegated to behind the loading docks, but Scott didn't feel like going out that way, and even if Sunny was political, he wasn't a snitch. They walked through the double glass doors, Scott carefully closing the inner lobby door behind him (God forbid a hint of smoke should drift into the office), and propped out the outer door with a handy cinderblock.

The air was sharp and cold, and as they walked to the parking lot their breath came out in puffs as if they had already lit up. He and Wan lit their cigarettes, and Scott had just begun to search his mind for small talk when the truck entered the parking lot.

The truck was the only vehicle Scott could see on this stretch of road and its engine, in bad repair, split the stillness of the night, sounding like a boiler on the point of exploding. Scott tensed. He knew the vehicles of nearly everyone on staff. The younger kids, who could afford them, drove Priuses. The older generation favored cheap sedans by Honda, Nissan, and Saturn. The few pickup trucks in use were vanity jobs, crisp, well-maintained suburban Rams. Nobody drove anything like the beast that idled before them, a hulking, battered old warhorse of a work truck. Whoever was behind the wheel had come with one intention: to make trouble. Probably a would-be vandal who hadn't expected to find anyone here. Now, the question was, would he turn tail and run or decide to make Sunny and Scott part of his message?

Scott turned to Sunny, who wore a dreamy smile, apparently unperturbed by the giant, looming truck. These fucking kids, Scott thought, and he could barely repress a shake of his head; they always thought they were so fucking safe. Sunny turned to Scott and, seeing he was on edge, shot him a grin that was probably meant to be reassuring. "Probably just needed to turn ar–"

The engine cut off in the middle of his sentence and Sunny shut up. The driver had left the lights on, pinning them in its beam like escaping prisoners caught in a spotlight as they cut across the yard. Scott racked his mind, trying to figure out what the hell The Telegraph had printed lately that could have pissed someone off so badly. There had been nothing but some fairly innocuous bullshit as far as Scott could remember.

Nothing disturbed the ominous silence that fell when the engine cut. Every instinct in Scott's body was telling him to run, but he was fairly sure that doing so would result in a bullet in his back. If Scott squinted he could just make out the shape of the man at the wheel. He was alone in the cab of the truck. A dark, broad-shouldered silhouette, hands gripping the steering wheel white-knuckle tight. He was shaking.

"What the fuck–" Sunny said, and then there was a cracking sound as the door opened. A smell of stale tobacco and sweat hit Scott from the cab as the form slid its bulk across the seat. For a moment the shape stood beside the truck, shrouded in darkness, and regarded them. Then it lunged, pulling something from under the seat; Scott caught the briefest glint of metal sliding out, and before he knew it, he had Sunny by the collar and was pulling him down and toward the only other car in the lot, Scott's own much-abused Volvo. It was yards away; there was no way they would make it to the scant protection it would provide. He tried to pull the unresisting Wan down for all the good it would do. They had missed their chance; it was hard to imagine easier targets.

It didn't matter. Scott heard the sound of the gun cocking and turned to look. The man had the barrel of what looked like a sawed-off shotgun nestled under his chin. Scott had turned just in time to watch him pull the trigger.

In the flash of the muzzle Scott saw the man's face for a split second before his head came apart like a smashed pumpkin. He was younger than Scott had expected, and his face bore a terrible look of resignation. Scott felt the warm unmistakable spray of blood hitting his face. The shock he had been fighting off since this whole unreal situation had begun overwhelmed him.

Some things you never get used to, he fuzzily reflected, as he began to wipe the stranger's blood from the lenses of his spectacles.

The next thing he knew, he was fishing for another cigarette.

~ ~ ~

After a couple of drags that passed in complete silence Scott managed to ask Sunny – if Scott was shocked, the younger man was positively traumatized – if he was all right. Sunny managed a slight nod, which Scott took as his cue to call the proper authorities: first Russell, and then the police.

He made his way to his car and took an old beach towel from the back seat. He wiped the worst of the blood off his face and then tossed the towel to Sunny, who stared blankly at it until Scott gave him a gentle prompting with a pantomime. Sunny began to rub vigorously at himself, as if he could scrub the night off of his skin.

By the time the flashing lights arrived, Scott had almost regained his equilibrium. A few patrol cars came first, cordoning off the crime scene, after doing a cursory check to make sure that neither of the dazed men sitting on the curb was bearing firearms. Satisfied that they were neither in danger nor posed a threat, the police went to their work. No further attention was paid to them as the police roped off the area and tried to block the worst of the gore from the view of the street. The paramedics arrived shortly after, and Scott couldn't help but give a wry chuckle as the junior partner, who looked all of twenty-two and distinctly green, performed what must have been the quickest signs-of-life check ever before turning his attention to Scott and Sunny.

After a quick check he pronounced them injury-free, but judged that Sunny was in minor shock. He cast a suspicious eye on Scott, as he apparently no longer exhibited any of the symptoms. Scott had to suppress another chuckle. Them's the breaks, kid, he thought ruefully. Stick around long enough and you'll get it.

After the paramedics arrived, Scott saw the man he was looking for. Detective Mark Quinn was a few years younger and a few pounds heavier than Scott. But they knew each other well, both from Scott's years on the crime beat and from sharing parallel stools at McCarthey's pub. They weren't exactly friends, but they were about as close to friends as Scott got to having these days, and he was happy to see Quinn was handling the case. He was peering into the dead man's truck, a manila envelope down by his side. He finished, turned, saw Scott, and with a wave began to walk towards him.

Scott stood and took a few strides forward, intercepting him in the parking lot. "Scott," Quinn said, voice tinged with sympathy, "Pretty rough night; you alright?"

Scott gave a stoic shrug, "I'll be fine, the kid's in rougher shape than I am. Any chance you'll send him on his way? He didn't see anything that I didn't see, and you can always question him later."

Quinn glanced over Scott's shoulder at Sunny. "Can he make it home alright?" Scott considered, then gave a nod. "Alright, let me just have a few words with him." He strode over to Sunny and introduced himself. Scott saw Sunny stand and weakly shake Quinn's hand. Scott couldn't exactly hear what Quinn was saying, but the low cadences of his speech told Scott that Quinn was in full cop patter mode – the lyrics might change but the song remained the same.

After a minute Sunny began to nod and Quinn passed him his card, Sunny stood up and started towards his own car. Scott nodded to him as he approached, but Sunny stopped and clasped his shoulder, a gesture that caught Scott off guard. He placed his own hand on top of Sunny's, "We'll talk later," he said as gently as he could. Sunny nodded, walked the rest of his way to his car, got behind the wheel and drove away. Scott watched him until he was out of sight.

Quinn was waiting for him when he turned back, "So why don't you tell me just what the hell happened here, Scott." Scott lit a cigarette – he had smoked nearly a third of the pack in thirty minutes and his throat felt like he had rubbed it with sandpaper, but he wanted it anyway – and began his story again. Quinn waited patiently, not interjecting until Scott came to a close: "What a mess."

Scott nodded, "Ayuh." He tried to leave it at that but could not quite help himself. "So just what the hell do you think happened?"

Quinn gave a shrug, "We'll find out, but for now, who knows? Maybe the guy had a grudge against the paper? Or maybe he was just some asshole who wanted to off himself but didn't want to join the choir invisible without an audience. Probably just some meth head who was driving by and saw you two open for business." There was a sudden, hopeful look in his eyes, "Is there any way that he could have done it by accident?" he asked, his voice suddenly eager. "Like he was aiming for you and lost control of the gun?"

Scott shook his head, "No, he had plenty of time. That shot went right where he meant it to, for sure and certain." Quinn nodded, disappointed, but before he could say anything more, an SUV entered the lot, driven by Russell. Russell was usually impeccably dressed and carried with him an air of paternal authority that was earned, not an affectation. But tonight he looked bewildered in the red and blue lights, his shock of gray hair uncombed, dressed in a Buffalo Bills T-shirt and a pair of dirty jeans that were obviously the first things in reach.

He parked his car across three spaces and shouted "Scott, just what the hell happened?" as he stepped out, sounding for all the world like he was calling after an errant deadline. When he got close enough, Scott began his story for the second time. Quinn let him go on uninterrupted again, probably using the opportunity to check his story for inconsistencies. When he finished, Russell's face was white. "Jesus," He managed to whisper. Then Quinn stepped in.

"We should have the identity of the man soon Mr. Russell, we'll need you to stay handy, tell us if you know him, or know any reason why he might do this." Russell gave a numb nod. Scott turned and headed towards the newsroom, front door still propped open by a cinderblock.

"Where the hell are you going?" Russell called.

"I'm going to write this up!" Scott called without stopping or turning.

"We already have half the run printed." Russell called.

"Well, call them and stop them before they finish the other half." Scott called, "People can't hear about this on the Channel 5 news, not if we want to be able to hold our heads up in public. The copy will be on your desk in twenty minutes."

~ ~ ~

Sunny spent the drive home wishing he had bummed another cigarette from Scott. His hands were shaking so badly that he had to grip the wheel until his fingers went white and numb to get them to stop. He stopped at an all-night Quikstop and bought his first pack since college. He had one in the parking lot, and then gave the rest of the pack to a homeless man sitting near the door.

He managed to drive the rest of the way home without getting in a wreck; the empty streets seemed to mock him with their placidity. It felt like disaster lurked just outside of his field of vision, that behind every quiet suburban door he passed, something unspeakable could be happening. He could not shake the feeling of being pursued, even as he pulled up to his apartment. He hurried up the steps and shoved his key in the door, forcing himself not to look behind him.

Only after the door was shut and the deadbolt locked could he even begin to calm himself down. He drew a deep breath and rested his head against the back of the door, closing his eyes and centering himself as best he could. "Alright," he said quietly to himself, "alright." He washed his face in the kitchen sink and began to undress, unbuttoning his shirt as he made his way to his bedroom.

Alicia had tried to wait up for him – the bedside light was on and an open Michael Chabon novel was splayed across her lap – but she had fallen asleep. Sunny stood in the doorway and watched her sleep. She snored softly, chest rising and falling, mouth open, exposing the right incisor that looked like a fang, red hair splayed out behind her. He watched her until he felt like himself again. He finished undressing before taking the book gently from her lap and placing it on the nightstand, brushing her cheek with his lips before he turned out the light. She smiled slightly in her sleep. It made Sunny feel very warm.

He hoped something mellow would help him sleep. He turned on Jackson Browne – Alicia slept so soundly that nothing short of a klaxon alarm could wake her once she was under – then slipped under the covers next to her.

Instinctively she drew closer to him, and he put his arm around her. Sunny stared up at the ceiling for a long time, and as he drifted off he was still wondering how the world that contained this moment could be the same one that contained what had happened in the parking lot. He wondered what the hell he was going to say when Alicia asked him how the night went.

~ ~ ~

His Army psych evaluation, which Spence had stolen out of curiosity, had noted in him "an abnormal, distinct inability to emphasize with others."

Spence had to admit that they had him there. The only part he objected to was the word "abnormal." In Spence's experience, a lack of empathy was one of the most uniform traits a person could have – the surest indicator of "normal" that he knew.

The psychiatrist went on to theorize that Spence was a budding sociopath or perhaps had undiagnosed Asperger syndrome. Spence wasn't sure about that, but he didn't really care one way or the other. Budding sociopath or no, the army had still deemed Spence fit to learn to shoot very big guns, blow shit up and kill a man with his hands. That had been all Spence was really interested in getting from them anyway.

What Spence knew that his profiler apparently didn't was that genetics was only part of the problem. Mental Illness, or "divergence," as they preferred to term it these days, could be taught.

Empathy could be beaten out of you.

He'd like to see his counselor get held down by four cackling fourteen-year-old boys while a fifth shoved dog shit into her mouth and then see her try to talk to Spence about empathy. Or to have to walk home three miles without your pants and shoes, face burning red all the way, the gooseflesh on your bird legs visible to anyone who cared to see in the cold autumn air. Aching testicles trying to draw into your stomach.

Then she could talk to him about anger issues.

The fact was that Spence had been scared more or less every day of his life. Or at least every day he could remember. Which amounted to the same thing.

On his 18th birthday he had enlisted in the Army, then Special Forces. A few dozen ways to kill imprinted in his instincts later, and suddenly Spence wasn't scared anymore.

Which wasn't to say that he still wasn't deeply fucked up.

He was.

There had been a few attempts at bonding in the Army. Attempts at what the CO called "unit cohesion."

It didn't take.

It didn't take long for Spence to realize he was broken, with all the deliberateness that the word implied.

He had *been* broken.

From there it took only a short extrapolation to realize that he would spend the rest of his life hurting as many people as possible.

The only question was, would he be an amateur? One of those faceless monsters who made people disappear into the back of their white van, until he was inevitably caught and dragged under the harsh fluorescent lights of some cheap courthouse to give the folks in the suburbs nightmares and the white trash a new focus of fascination? Put on display like a freak until their morbid curiosity was exhausted and he was finally dragged into some dank prison to wait for the needle? Or would he make his condition work for him, and kill for fun and profit?

After his four-year tour and surprise bonus round of stop loss he took his show on the road. He had decided on fun and profit.

At the moment, though, he was strictly working for fun. Blowing off some steam in an unforeseen intermission. Technically he was on the clock. He had a target. He had waited all night for the target at their home. The target hadn't shown.

It was all right, he didn't think the target had been tipped. He'd just have to come back tomorrow morning and shove the target's head in the oven then.

But it was irritating, like having blue balls, having come so close to violence and been forced to pull back. And like blue balls, you couldn't focus on anything else until the problem had been taken care of. It was just too distracting. So now he was looking for something to help take his mind off it – nothing with a body count, just a little something to ease the pressure.

There were plenty of candidates. It was just closing time and the streets were teeming with the drunk and deserving. But they all seemed so mundane, so unaware. As challenging to the palate as vanilla soft-serve ice cream. He wanted someone really enriching.

That was when he spotted the yellow Hummer with the "Support Our Troops" yellow ribbon.

That's a bingo.

He slid his anonymous black sedan a few spaces farther down the block. Then he parked got out of the car and discreetly taped a piece of cardboard over his license plate. He leaned against his car and waited.

The Hummer's lights flashed and made an annoying electronic squelching sound. Spence head darted towards the sound as looked for his quarry.

He was easy to spot. Drunkenly weaving towards the Hummer. Holding out his arm with the keys in hand, as if he were blind and resting his hand on the shoulder of the invisible man who was leading him. He wore mandals and three days of stubble. Spence was reasonably sure that he'd lost his backwards baseball cap somewhere over the course of the night. Everything about him was detestable. Two shapes trailed dutifully behind him. There was something in their walk, a pent-up energy: They weren't getting laid tonight, and they'd be looking to let out the energy elsewhere.

Spence smiled slightly and congratulated himself on selecting such a fine object for his aggression.

He crouched down and unfolded a pocketknife – not big enough to scare off his quarry or his two bros – and began to chip away at the bumper sticker, careful to fillet away as much yellow paint as he could. The paint flaked away like scales coming off grilled salmon.

The kid had no fucking survival skills whatsoever. He didn't even see what Spence was doing until he was less than twenty yards away. When he did, he gave a great wounded bellow, as if he had stepped on a nail. "Hey MOTHERFUCKER!" he screamed.

Spence obliged, acting the part. He flinched and dropped the knife where it clattered on the pavement and gleamed in the low sodium light. He pressed himself against the back of the car, the one direction he couldn't escape, as if the metal might suddenly swallow him up. It drew them in.

It wouldn't have been hard to trap them even if their tempers hadn't been inflamed with booze and frustration. Spence was not an intimidating man. His build was slight, his face far from hard. He bore the watery, colorless eyes, receding hairline and thin mouth of a high school math teacher. Signs of weakness excited this type, he knew from experience. He felt them press in.

"The fuck you think you're doing?" the lead asked as he shoved Spence hard against the car. If it felt odd to the quarry when his fingers found taut muscle on Spence's chest instead of the soft flesh his hands were expecting, he was too drunk to listen to his instincts. Even if he had, the cringing flinch Spence gave would have set him off.

"Fucking up a man's car like that. What are you, stupid?" The one on his right wearing a Tapout shirt asked.

There was Spence's cue. "No," he said, and there was no flinch in his voice. As he stood straight, bracing his legs for maximum torque he saw something unmistakable: the confused beginnings of fear in their eyes. It felt good; it felt fucking narcotic.

Before the quarry could say anything, Spence had broken his elbow. Before he could scream Spence had kicked his kneecap with as much force as he dared and felt it give way agreeably beneath his boot. For the *piece de résistance* Spence grabbed the hair at the back of the boy's head and brought his forehead down hard against the bumper as he fell. Before he slumped to the ground, even before he saw the red smear against the yellow, Spence knew he had damaged the boy a lot more than he had meant to. Neither of his buddies moved against him. They didn't even run. Spence had hit them someplace that was even more primal than flight or fight. A place where the overriding survival instinct was "Maybe if I don't move he won't see me and I won't get eaten."

Spence bent down and scooped up the pocketknife, then made for the car without turning to look at either of the stunned friends. They didn't so much as call after him.

Spence drove three blocks, pulled over and removed the cardboard covering his plates. He was five miles away by the time he heard the news break on the scanner.

He made his way through out of the city towards the suburbs. He would go again to the target's house and complete the contract, then drive straight on through the night until he hit Santa Barbara. He was reasonably sure that he had made a clean getaway, but why chance things? At the very least there would be complications, and that was the one thing a man in his profession couldn't afford to deal with.

He saw the blue and red lights flashing off the stucco walls just as he rounded the corner. It was too late to stop or turn around without being completely obvious, so he slowed his car and hoped he didn't look as conspicuous as he felt. He cursed aloud as he passed the three patrol cars that were parked in front of his target's house. No way to know what happened, but given the number of cops swarming around the place and the stare that the hawk-faced patrol cop stationed at the edge of the front yard gave him, he could guess that it was serious.

Keeping his cool, Spence passed the spectacle and tried to make it out of the suburbs. Apparently going out for a bit of night air had saved as well as fucked him. Spence's life had been filled with odd moments of double-edged serendipity like that. In his distraction he nearly turned down a cul-de-sac. Cursing, he corrected course at the last second, before finally finding a straightaway that led out of the suburb.

He made his way back to his motel room, taking the backstreet routes he had mapped in advance to avoid detection. He made it back without seeing another patrol car. He went to his room and closed the door, undressed, and set his alarm for six o'clock, less sleep than he would have liked to operate on. Tomorrow was sure to be one hell of a day. But the news would come on at six, the local papers too, and he'd have a chance to figure out what caused this mess and how he was going to get out of it. Things had gotten very complicated.

He lay on the stiff motel bed and closed his eyes. He fell asleep almost immediately.

~ ~ ~

Jonathan Pike had given up on sleep that night. There was far too much at stake and far too much of it was out of his hands for any chance at peace of mind.

He was good and fucked with no real options, and he had no one to blame for being in that state but himself. He sat on his porch, a mostly untouched cigar smoldering in the ashtray and a glass of strong unwatered bourbon beside him. The view from his home, built high on a hilltop on his ranch, gave him a 360-degree view of his holdings. It was the heart of the empire that he had built out of a hundred acres of cow shit.

And he was at the risk of losing it all. For what? For the crime of misjudging two men? It all seemed so grotesquely unfair.

That the first of those men was his son made the whole thing even bitterer. That his own flesh and blood would be the instrument of his downfall was almost too much to bear. It drove him crazy. He knew that the fault was partially his; that he had no one but himself to blame for how his son turned out. He should have taken a stronger hand with the boy, been more involved in his raising, or at the very least kept a tighter leash on the boy when it became clear just what he was becoming.

But damn it, even as a child the boy had shown so little ambition and even less aptitude. He was slow of mind and slovenly of body; he showed interest in nothing aside from pleasure. There was precious little in him that interested Pike. He just seemed like he wasn't worth the effort.

Pike idly wondered if his own father ever felt the same despair towards him that Pike felt for his son. It would be of a different caste; no one would ever accuse Pike of being unmotivated. But Pike thought that the taste of the despair, that sense of being unable to recognize any of oneself in their own child, would be similar. Pike's father had regarded Pike the way a coyote who had somehow given birth to a timber wolf might regard its cub. It wasn't that Pike's father was a soft man– far from it; he wasn't above doling out a beating, or a harsh threat in order to keep his workers in line or his enemies at bay. He had made the family money by renting out his modest ranch to moonshiners for their stills and stashes, and he had been crafty enough to put that money into buying yet more land, rather than squandering it on material pleasures the way so many of his generation had.

But he had not had any of Pike's viciousness. If his father had an enemy, he would face him and beat him until he gave up. If Pike had an enemy, he always made sure the man who fancied himself his enemy would never have a chance to act as one again. Killing them tended to be the most efficient way of accomplishing this. As far as he knew, Pike's father had never killed a man. Pike lived his life by the phrase "By any means necessary," and as a result his wealth and influence stretched past boundaries that his father never dreamed of.

His father would hamstring a man.

Pike would set the dogs on him while he was down.

He had no squeamishness in him. His son was something else – all squeamishness, soft even in his venality. Pike would just as soon have no part of him.

Well, ignoring the runt had finally cost him; the son of a bitch had finally shit the bed on a large enough scale that a few payoffs in the right places, and several more severe steps beyond that, couldn't cover it. He had endangered everything. Now he was in Europe, probably slammed out of his mind on club drugs, in too much of a stupor to even be aware of how much shit he had caused. And Pike was still cleaning up his mess. Or to, be more accurate, the mess the mess had made.

Now this one Pike found hard to put on his own shoulders; all he was guilty of was trusting his people to do their jobs. Was that so wrong? Was it truly too much to ask for a little fucking competence? Let alone a little fucking loyalty?

But no, one of Pike's men, a boy really, had started making threats. What's worse, he seemed to have evidence to back those threats up. Pike didn't know what, but it was enough to worry Bingham, and Bingham didn't worry easily.

Pike was firmly of the philosophy that if you wanted something done right you should do it yourself. But the boy was too close to Pike for him to be able to handle this in-house. Bingham had set up the whole thing, found a contractor to come in and take care of the situation nice and quietly, accidental death all the way. Less suspicious than a nun in church, or so he had been assured. What was really bothering Pike was that he was relying on a variable. That he had not been able to look into the eyes of the man who right now, at this very moment, held his fate in his hands, and see if he was worth a bucket of warm spit. He was being forced to rely on other peoples' judgment. Forced to let other people decide his fate.

And there was nothing that Pike hated more.

He was a builder, and he hadn't made his place in the world by sitting back and letting others make his decisions for him. He stirred his drink and contemplated the dark horizon.

The phone in his pocket rang. Pike gave a sigh of relief, at last it was over. He picked up the phone and waited to be told that everything was done. That he could finally rest easy.

Instead he was informed that he had misjudged yet another pair of men. Sorely.

~ ~ ~

Scott had finished the story and had gone over his account again with Quinn, and then a fourth time with another policeman. Russell told him not to worry about coming in the next day – now technically *this* day – and Scott thanked him and took his leave.

He drove alone to the trailer park where he lived, weaving his way through the narrow streets, before parking in front of the small home. He walked into the foyer which doubled as a living room. There was no carpeting, just a series of rugs that Scott had thrown down to cover the linoleum, and they were covered with cigarette ash and burns. There were no pictures on the wall, just a few bookcases and a coffee table in the middle of the room, which held a small square TV flanked by beer bottles and a couple of brimming ashtrays. He made his way through to the kitchen, took a large water glass, filled it with ice and then covered the ice in Bushmills. He took the drink out to the small back porch, and sat on a wicker chair with a heavy sigh. He had put up a small bamboo blind that gave him a measure of privacy on the raised porch, but still afforded him a view.

He sipped at his whiskey and watched the horizon, getting up to refill his drink once before the sun went up.

It was all fucked up. He knew that was an understatement, but he felt instinct telling him that he was underestimating just how fucked up this was. He didn't know what the story would be on John Doe; if they had identified him by the time Scott had left, no one had bothered to tell him about it. But he seriously doubted that whatever the initial story would be would express the depth and breadth of what was fucked up either. This was some serious shit, no two ways about it, the most serious that he had been in for quite some time. Scott sat and watched the horizon and sipped his whiskey until his head swam with it. The rising sun basked everything in a sickly pink light, as he tried to decide just what the hell he was going to do about it.

~ ~ ~

The sunlight danced playfully on the waves as they lapped mere yards from Amanda Vasquez's back porch. Which she, a pretty Latina with a dark complexion, deep brown eyes and Bettie Page bangs, surveyed with quiet satisfaction, a cup of coffee warming her hands against the cool ocean breeze. A beachfront condo. That was all Amanda had to think to calm any anxiety that crept into her mind. Friends all getting married and having kids? Beachfront condo. Job not going exactly as she foresaw it? Beachfront condo. Afraid what finding herself back in San Rita meant? Beachfront condo.

It was on the wrong beach, true, and she had to share the place with a roommate to make it work, but still those four syllables were immutable and they calmed her like a mantra.

Her condo was nestled on the northern beach of San Rita, known to the locals as Elmo's Beach. As a rule the southern and recently remodeled Avalon Beach got all the sun, surf and tourist money, while Elmo's got the fog, drunks on ATVs carousing around the dunes at all hours, embittered fishermen, and the occasional meth cooks who made use of the thick woods that bordered San Rita on the north end, but a beach was a beach, and Amanda finally had her piece.

Her people had always been shunted to the east end of San Rita, as far from the beaches and as close to the fields as possible. San Rita was a small city, just under a hundred thousand if you counted a few of its bordering suburbs, but just large enough that it could get away with such segregation without being too conspicuous. Twenty-five years ago San Rita had been just another blue-collar beach town, when without warning it suddenly became the premier destination for retirees and moneyed folk who couldn't quite swing Montecito. Before you knew it, real estate shot so high that no one who made less than six figures a year could afford to own a home. The few families and ranchers who owned land pre-boom kept their cool, cattlemen heads and made a killing. Now, after ten years of careful management – some would say exploitation – San Rita had become the jewel of the Central Coast of California; bordered by beaches on its north and south end, fertile agricultural land on its east, and the beginnings of the Big Sur wilderness a mere fifteen minutes north. Host to a popular college, a downtown that kept the wheels of the economy turning with boutique stores during the day, and a long row of bars that kept things busy all night. It regularly made the kind of lists you saw clogging up Yahoo and MSN. "7 Best Places To Retire" "9 Best Unspoiled Spots On The Pacific."

All powered by a working class that got shunted just outside the city limits, so they could drive to town every day and keep the service economy rolling. Someone had to clean up the dog shit in utopia and you couldn't have the people who did it actually live there. Keep them outside of the dream with just enough of a sniff of it to keep them begging to get in, with never a chance of it actually happening.

Those had been her parents. Her father was a migrant laborer who had found steady work in the vineyards. Her mother a maid in one of the earliest resort hotels. They had gotten together through the church and were married by a priest without appearing in the county's records. They managed to buy a little house on the city's outskirts, the house where Amanda and her brother had grown up together, and where her parents still lived.

Amanda was bright, both her parents had seen it, and in order to nurture that brightness while avoiding further entanglement with the system, they had enrolled her and her brother in private Catholic school at great personal sacrifice. It had paid off. First the nuns and then a wider array of teachers, coaches and counselors had also noticed and nurtured that brightness. They had put Amanda in Honors Everything and by the time she was in high school had her fast on the track for a couple dozen scholarships, both academic and athletic (cross country in the fall, basketball in the winter, track in the spring). Again, it had paid off. Thirteen years after being enrolled in their kindergarten, Amanda graduated from St. Rita College Preparatory, valedictorian, on her way to Harvard in the fall. She had been the feel-good story that graduation season, showing up in every paper including the one she now worked for, beaming proudly, holding her diploma. The child of migrant workers now bound for the finest the Ivy League elite had to offer. Horatio Alger would have shit himself. But after four years of grueling study, Amanda had done something that had *really* shocked people.

She'd come back.

New York, Los Angeles, Washington, D.C., maybe even a spot on one of the European desks. All of these possibilities had been predicted for her by proud teachers and mentors. With her talent, drive and charisma she could have gone anywhere. The idea that she would come back to the by-turns scruffy and gentrified little beach town and work for the small paper there had never even entered the equation.

But for Amanda there had never been any other option.

It had been the fault of the nuns really. Well, one particular nun. Sister Agnes who had above the whiteboard of her third grade class hung a sign with the Gandhi quote that read "Be The Change You Wish to See in the World" The quote had hit Amanda's burgeoning conscience with the force of a bullet and lodged itself there. It became the grain of sand that was necessary for her pearl of a mind to grow around. She had never spoken to anyone about the importance of the quote to her. Had never exploited it as the basis for a scholarship essay or dissertation. Instead she had kept it private, in a little chamber she hid in her heart where it burned within her.

In her time she had seen missing blond-haired blue-eyed college girls get front-page stories, while girls who went missing from her neighborhood had to deal with a few inches of ink on page A12, if they were lucky enough to be noticed at all. San Rita ran on cheap uncomplaining labor provided by the disenfranchised and the easily ignored. All the smiles and sunshine masked a lot of sweat and no small amount of blood. Interviews were given to civic leaders with no questions asked about the conditions of the migrant camps they ran. Once a boy had been hit outside on her street by a man driving a BMW. The boy didn't have papers, the man did. The incident never appeared in the paper.

That would be what Amanda would change in the world.

Whenever she had talked about this, always in careful abstracts, with dorm mates or students, they would brush her off, saying that it was just the old Catholic guilt raising its head. Amanda preferred to think of it as her duty. She would not be one of those people who forgot where they came from, who turned their back on who they were. A community had raised her, a community had given her opportunity. She had a duty to that community. Even if that duty was to wake it the fuck up.

So she had come back, ready and railing to fight the power and then ... and then not much. She had spent almost two years covering community events, and writing op eds at Christmas. The closest she had gotten to controversy was when she had covered a city council meeting about the allocations for new stop signs. It wasn't as if she had time to develop stories on her own either. She was being kept busy; it was just that she was being kept busy with meaningless junk work.

It wasn't, as she knew some must think, that she didn't mind paying her dues, or that she was used to being a star. She knew the value of proving oneself by performing exceptional work on unexceptional tasks. The fact that she had to make her bones didn't bother her. It was the fact that, for the first time in her life, she was doing less than she was capable of.

As she dressed and drove from the beachfront, across town to the industrial outskirt where the paper was based, she told herself that she'd confront Russell today if there wasn't something meatier than a dog show on her desk. Of course, she told herself that most mornings. But she may have finally hit saturation. One never knew.

She parked and walked towards The Telegraph's offices. The squat building was made of cinder blocks and glass, and did little to differentiate itself from the paint store on the left or the cabinet shop on the right. She passed through the two sets of glass doors and found herself in the bullpen, an agreeable buzz of activity having already been reached at nine. Everyone was in their own orbits, talking to each other or into the ends of phones.

Stepping onto the floor was not unpleasantly like finding oneself in a beehive: Too busy ceaselessly functioning to even notice you until you stepped in and became a part of it.

Gary, the gray-faced front desk man, nodded almost imperceptibly to her as she passed, and then spoke, something he had only done perhaps half a dozen times since she had begun working here over a year and a half ago. She was so surprised that it took her a second to realize that she had not heard what he had actually said.

She stopped walking and turned to Gary. "Come again?" she asked.

Gary sighed as if some great task was being asked of him, and then in a voice that sounded like matchsticks breaking, croaked, "Russell would like a word in his office," before turning back to contemplate the front door like a Buddha.

She kept walking, trying not to show the nervous energy that her brain buzzed with, the way it always did when the path forward wasn't immediately clear. She had wanted a conversation, but she had wanted it on her own terms – to be the one laying the ambush, not the one walking into it. What the hell could it be about? She stopped at her desk and dumped off her purse. She stopped for a moment, took a breath and then got her brain to shut up. It was one of her best skills, the ability to center and take whatever was in front of her. It was one of the reasons she'd been able to succeed.

She made her way across the bullpen, the large clamorous floor where most of the reporters did their work in cubicles now bustling with early-morning activity and din, to the narrow hallway where half a dozen small editors' offices lay in a cluster like grapes, framed front pages of big events between them. Russell's was at the end of the hall, the stem at the top of the grape bunch. Amanda took a moment, steeled herself and knocked. "Come in!" he called, in his rough bark.

Russell sat behind his desk. He looked tired, his ruddy face unusually pale, his hair missing its trademark oil. He looked up at Amanda, blinked a few times behind the square grandpa glasses that he only wore in his office, and then looked back down at the papers he'd been studying. This was a typical greeting from Russell, who had acted grandfatherly for the first two weeks she had worked at the paper, and then, as soon as he realized she wouldn't break, dealt with her in the same brusque manner with which he dealt with everyone else. With his Just for Men colored hair and big steam shovel hands, Amanda couldn't help but like him. He exuded an easy authority, the kind of which very few of the men of her generation seemed aware, let alone capable.

"You're handling crime beat today," he said.

For the second time that day, Amanda was having trouble believing what she heard. "What about Molina?" she asked, referring to the grim, exceedingly taciturn man who usually handled that job. Russell glanced up at her coolly, with a gaze that was meant to make Amanda think he was having second thoughts. Amanda held it; she always made sure she knew what she was getting into.

"Scott has the day off," Russell said, "due to his involvement in last night's events."

Amanda was taken aback, "What events?"

Russell rolled his eyes and sighed, "Some reporter." He launched into the story; Amanda managed to keep her cool, or at least her mouth from falling open. "So," he summarized, "you'll be filing the copy today, and maybe tomorrow, should Mr. Molina need an extra day to ..." here he faltered for just one moment; Amanda wouldn't have noticed if she wasn't a keen listener, "deal with the stress." He concluded, "Any further questions?"

She shook her head, "Good, the police log is on your desk, copy will be due at five. From what I understand it's been a pretty eventful night. I know I don't have to tell you this, but I'll go ahead and recommend that you check out the frat boy case first. Everyone loves a good story about a frat boy getting roughed up. The college kids and the gentry like to know we're paying attention, and the townies like to live vicariously." He smiled at his own joke, then nodded to the door. Amanda nodded and left the room. She managed not to skip down the hallway.

Ask and you will receive. Here was the crack she had needed. Sure, it was temporary, and she was still stuck writing about white people, but Molina wouldn't be around forever, and they had come to her first. It was time for Amanda to do what she did best: to show what she was capable of.

~ ~ ~

It was two o'clock in the afternoon when the knock came on Sunny Wan's door. He had no idea who it could be. After he had told her about what had happened and assured her he was all right, Alicia had left for her job at the bookstore, and she wouldn't be back until five. He had spoken to a uniformed policeman that morning, after which Russell had given him a call, his gruff manner dropping just enough to ask if Sunny was all right. He had assured Russell that he was. Russell had hung up, and Sunny had spent the remainder of the day finding that it was absolutely impossible to concentrate on anything.

He felt wired on a kind of nervous energy that he could put to no good use, nor even an indifferent one. He couldn't write, couldn't garden. Trying to put any focus on a book or film was also proving to be an impossibility. Even the constant array of stimuli provided by his Xbox couldn't distract him for long. He had gone from pacing and fervently wishing he could go to the corner store to buy cigarettes, to pacing and fighting the temptation to go to the store and buy cigarettes. As far as he could tell that would be how he would spend the remainder of the day, until the knock on the door came.

Whoever Wan had expected, Scott Molina staring at him through red-rimmed eyes on his doorstep had not been it.

"Hey," he said, "you get lunch yet?" Sunny shook his head. "Feel like stepping out?"

"Very much so," Scott nodded and turned began walking towards his beater car. Sunny grabbed a hoodie off the rack by the door and started after him.

~ ~ ~

They ended up at The Establishment. A brick-and-mortar place that lay between the two main streets of San Rita's shopping district, far enough off the beaten pub path to remain a local joint, its clientele a little too old to be considered a townie one. A group of slightly seedy-looking men smoked outside next to the big oak tree in front of the place, dropping their butts into the gutter and planter box when they finished. Scott nodded to them as they entered; they nodded back.

Scott chose a booth near the back and, without looking at the menu, ordered a burger and a tall beer from a waitress in her fifties who appeared beside the table so suddenly it was if she had been conjured, before Sunny even had a chance to sit down. Sunny glanced at the menu, then figured if Scott knew the place so well he must know what was good. He ordered the same burger but subbed in a Coke, an action that caused Scott to crook his eyebrow.

The waitress reappeared shortly with a sweating beer that looked just over thirty-two ounces, Sunny's Coke dwarfed beside it. Scott took a long pull off of it, giving a little unconscious sigh of satisfaction, then looked up at

Sunny and spoke for the first time since appearing at his door.

"Sorry, about dropping by unannounced, I would have called but I didn't have your number."

Sunny nodded while wondering just who the hell's phone number Scott *would* have – the man turned being a loner into an art form, "That's alright," Sunny said, "I'm glad you did, I needed to get out of the house anyway." Scott nodded, and Sunny was about to thank him for what he did the other night, but he interrupted.

"Did it seem right to you? What happened last night?"

Sunny was taken aback, he almost laughed, "Ah, no. In fact I'd go so far as to say someone shooting themselves at my work place is about as close to my personal definition of wrong as you're liable to get."

Scott waved his hand; he seemed disappointed. "That's not what I mean. It just feels like there oughta be more."

Sunny shrugged, "Maybe there will be, they haven't released the guy's name yet."

"Oh, I know who it is." Scott muttered.

"You do?" Sunny said, unable to hide his surprise

Scott looked up at him and met his eyes with something that was close to a challenge, "Yeah, I know who it'll be. Loner, down on his luck. He looked a bit young to be a vet, but they'll find something to wrap it up. Maybe he lost his job or got divorced. Something that they can point to and say, 'Well of course he snapped.' Trust me, by the time that story makes it out of the San Rita P.D., it'll be well cooked. All Russell will have to do is print the denouement in tomorrow's paper and we can all move on with our lives."

"And you don't want that?" Sunny asked slowly. Scott took another long pull on his drink, though this time he didn't give the sigh of satisfaction. Instead he fixed his eyes on Sunny again. It was like looking into the eyes of a hawk with cataracts – something not as sharp and clear as it once was, but still dangerous all the same.

"Let me ask you. Why do it?"

"Why kill yourself? God, who knows?"

"No, why kill yourself *there*. At the newspaper."

"Someone's mad about something we printed? Maybe a grudge against Russell? One of the owners?"

Scott slapped his palm down on the table in frustration, not loud enough for the others in the restaurant to notice, but the suddenness of the action made Sunny start a little, "You're thinking like they want you to. Forget that it's *our* newspaper. Go more general, think of it as *a* newspaper. Here you are, it's the last thing you're ever going to do. You assume that you want some privacy, that way no one tries to stop you, or if you botch it you don't make the last thing you see a bunch of people watching you choke on your own blood. Instead you drive out to a public place where any number of variables could happen, and not just any public place, but a public place whose function it is to spread information. Now why the hell do you do that?"

"Because you want someone to notice." Sunny answered.

Scott cocked his finger like a gun while he took another sip of his beer. It was now half empty. "Bingo," he said when he finished.

Sunny considered it for a moment and then shook his head, "But there's something you haven't considered."

Scott looked up at him and frowned, "What's that?"

"Who is going to notice him if he kills himself here, who wouldn't if he killed himself anywhere else?" Sunny asked, "I mean, you off yourself in public, it gets noticed a little quicker, granted. Your landlady doesn't find you after you've been dead two weeks and half-eaten by your dog. But anyone who knew you, who would matter enough to this guy that he wants to send a message to them, would find out eventually. Why go to all that trouble to move that schedule up a few days? I mean who would notice that this guy was dead who wouldn't have if he'd killed himself by jumping off a bridge?"

The question was punctuated by the arrival of their food, which the waitress set before them with a ceremonial thud. The burger did look good, Sunny had to admit, even if it was so rare that it was bleeding out on his steak fries. Scott killed the rest of his drink with one last swallow; the waitress took it to refill without being asked. Scott took a bite of his burger and chewed for a moment before swallowing and answering, "I can think of a couple of people who wouldn't have noticed it otherwise."

"Who?" Sunny asked.

"Newsmen."

~ ~ ~

Amanda was having her lunch at the Down Street Deli, a semi-bohemian place that offered their specialty sandwiches at 4.20, and piled the meats, cheeses and veggies on so thick that they singlehandedly kept large portions of the student body it was so popular with from malnutrition. Old-timey signs advertising candy, tobacco and soft drinks for a few cents each lined the walls. Legitimate antiques – none of the mass-produced stuff that was supposed to lend an air of authenticity for the irony deficient. The Old Crow Medicine Show played over a pair of tinny overhead speakers, barely rising over the rattling isolating fan. Amanda had a copy of the night's police reports fanned out before her on the tabletop, which was balanced on top of a barrel. She leaned forward on her stool, sipping her green tea. This whole thing was weird.

Like any city that made a lot of its money off of the bars, San Rita had its fair share of closing-time violence. Patrons who decided to tenderize each other before walking home for the night. Townies stomping a college boy who'd gotten a bit too familiar. College kids working over a townie who'd been a bit too free with one of their girls. Fights over unpaid tabs, fights over bets, fights over women, fights over whether the band had played too loud, fights over whether or not Zeppelin sucked or ruled, fights over whether the Earth went around the sun or vice versa, fights over just about anything. But this was different.

For one thing, no one seemed to know just where the attacker fit into the great San Rita ecosystem. The witnesses said that he was older, and the strange, anonymous-looking sketch that the police had drawn up showed someone who was well into his thirties, with a slightly receding hairline and round spectacles that made him look owlish being the only distinguishing features. He wasn't a student, but he wasn't one of the regulars either; the middle-aged barfly community was relatively small in this town and they tended to stick to their own watering holes away from the meat-market action that the main strip of bars on Maria St. provided. No one could quite figure out what this guy was even doing out at two AM.

The viciousness of the attack was odd too. This wasn't the matter of some missing teeth and a couple of broken ribs. The kid was in a coma with his brain swelling against the sides of his skull, fit to burst. The doctors were doubtful at best about his prospects of coming out of it.

"Such violence in our fair community. I never thought I would see the day." She looked up to see Colin McNamara looking over her shoulder, wearing his trademark smirk and a black T-shirt cut to show off his biceps and bull neck, "I'm shocked that such dastardly mayhem would occur outside one of our proud public houses. Truly it is a blight." He circled around the table and sat down, "I'm surprised such a periodical of note would even deign to print such sordid news. This is the sort of thing one would expect to see in the pages of Mr. Hearst's Yellow Periodicals. I thought you guys were mostly concerned with youth soccer, and how great growth is."

"You notice how I haven't responded to you?" Amanda asked.

Colin's face fell in an exaggerated frown, "Oh come on, Mandy." There were few things that Amanda hated more than being called Mandy – blame Barry Manilow and catty 9th grade girls for that one – which Colin was well aware of. "Is that anyway to talk to someone you've known since small times?"

They had indeed known each other since small times. Colin had been Amanda's classmate at San Rita Catholic School from second grade until he had moved to the public San Rita High School in freshman year. Small times wasn't the problem. The problem was that after coming back from college, feeling strangely adrift in her hometown and looking for something familiar to latch onto, she had latched onto Colin. The following three months were what she considered to be easily the biggest mistake in her young life.

She looked up and glared at him, "What exactly do you want?" Amanda asked, "Because if you're about to say conversation, then we both know that's a damn lie."

Colin held up his hands in mock surrender, "Well a little catching up was really what I had in mind, but I have to admit I have the slightest of ulterior motives."

"Uh-huh."

"I just want a look at that," he said, pointing down at the police report.

Amanda felt herself bristle. "Those are open records, why not go request them yourself?"

Colin grinned, "Open records they may be, but the cops always seem to find some perfectly valid bureaucratic reason not to give them to me. They don't really like me down there, as you know."

Colin had been an academy student for six months before dropping out and going into business for himself as a private operator. The ones he'd been training with took it as a betrayal; the ones who had already been in the department took it as a sign of weakness. Either way, it had won him no friends in the SRPD.

"Why, are you interested?" Amanda sighed.

"The parents of the kid who got roughed up hired me to look into it. For some reason they don't have all that much faith in the cops' ability to, you know, solve shit, despite the fancy Prowlers and all." He spoke with a thick Boston accent so it came out "Prawhler." Since his parents had gotten divorced in fourth grade, Colin had spent every summer back East in Boston. He had a slight accent as a result, but he played it up to "intimidate the left coasters," as he liked to say. He didn't ease up as he continued, "I'm following my own leads but it doesn't hurt to see what the opposition knows."

They called Amanda's name. He held up a finger, went to the counter and paid for her veggie sandwich and his own hot pastrami. He handed Amanda her sandwich, then unwrapped and bit into his own with a gusto that bordered on unseemly before continuing the conversation, "So whatdoya say? All I'm asking is that you let me, a public citizen, take a look at public information. There's nothing there that could be construed as an ethical breach, even for one as scrupulous as yourself."

"I'll let you see if you promise to stop talking like an extra from *The Departed*."

"Done," he responded in his flat West Coast voice.

Amanda hesitated, then passed the report across the table before unwrapping her sandwich and taking a bite. She knew she was being played, but she couldn't see the harm in him taking a look. Besides, Colin might be a shit boyfriend, but he was a good investigator. Not only did he probably have a better chance at solving this thing than the cops did, but he would be a valuable source of information in the future, when Amanda started playing for higher stakes. Say what you would about him, but Colin could be depended on to repay a favor.

Amanda watched as he brusquely flipped through the report, his eyes scanning quickly across the lines of information, most of which Amanda had a feeling he already knew. Her instincts seemed correct as the document proved not to be worthy of his full attention.

"Since when have you been working crime beat?" he asked.

"I'm not, they just have me filling in for Mr. Molina."

Colin smirked at the prefix, and Amanda blushed, but he didn't mention it. "Oh, is he *sick*?" he asked, crooking his elbow and making the glugluglug motion.

As a Catholic, Latina and Journalist, Amanda had an instinct about closing ranks against outsiders. She bristled at the implication, even though the rumors of Scott's alcoholism had reached even she, who purposefully kept out of office politics. She was surprised Colin hadn't heard about the shooting at the newspaper, but she figured she'd given him enough information for the day,

"No," she said stiffly, "There's been a flu bug going around the office. It was Scott's turn, is all."

Colin looked up at her and gave the confident self-satisfied grin that charmed his way into so many girls' panties, but now just made Amanda want to hit him.

"Well, if you're their go-to girl now, you can expect to cover the crime desk on a fairly regular basis. From what I hear, old 'Mister' Molina is sick an awful lot." With that, he shoved the last quarter of his sandwich into his mouth, then stood up and left the table with a playful bow. The screen door snapped shut behind him.

~ ~ ~

The diner that Spence waited in was fashioned from an Airstream trailer, its walls decorated, somewhat redundantly, in Spence's opinion with pictures of the same Airstream trailer in its glory days, people posing in front of it smiling and waving, as if to say, "Wow this is quite an Airstream trailer." Spence failed to see the cause for such excitement. The trailer sat in a deeply wooded lot. It was technically out of The San Rita city limits, situated in The Six Cities, or what the local townie wits referred to as "The Shit Cities" a grouping of rural communities that were not technically part of San Rita but whose citizenry and community affairs were so inbred with it that they looked like an Appalachian family tree.

Spence had positioned himself at the end of the trailer. The waitress had poured him a single cup of coffee that had now been empty for five full minutes.

The wait was over. Spence's client entered the diner as a king enters court. It was the first time Spence had seen Pike in the flesh: A powerfully built man in his early sixties who wore a long white drooping mustache and string tie. Both were for show; San Rita hadn't been so shit-kicker as to have string ties actually in fashion since before the man was born. But it behooved his client to posture himself as a link to San Rita's mythical past; one that he had never been a part of, if it had in fact existed.

After the waitress had rushed to greet him and he had dismissed her with a kiss on the cheek, he scanned the diner, found Spence and strode down its length in a way that wasn't exactly friendly. A huge bodyguard with a shaved head squeezed through the narrow door to follow in his wake, along with the man who had hired Spence, a ginger retired biker named Bingham Earle, who was apparently the old man's number one lieutenant. Spence supposed it was hard to find good help these days.

The two booths behind Spence's were empty, the one across the aisle from him occupied by a kid who had come in after Spence, now engrossed in his iPod and gyro. Pike slid into the booth with a grunt. The bodyguard stood to attention beside him. Bingham positioned himself on Spence's side of the booth, staring down at Spence and trying his darnedest to intimidate him. The waitress brought Pike's coffee, was forced to refill Spence's, and took the old man's order of linguiça and eggs.

"Now, son," the man said, the feigned folksiness of his voice matching the string tie, "Why don't you just tell me what the hell happened here." His tone was light, but his eyes glittered with repressed violence.

Spence spoke in the calm, flat voice he used for delivering bad news and no options, "I waited at the target's home. When he didn't appear I went out looking for him. He apparently took a detour."

The old man looked down his nose at Spence, peering with exaggerated shock, "A detour, huh? I suppose that is one way to put it." He took a sip from his coffee. "Did it ever occur to you that I hired you to neutralize that man to prevent exactly such a thing as what has happened from happening?"

"That wasn't my fault. I told you to tell me anything that might be a variable with this client. If he had a history of depression or mental illness, I should have been told."

The man gave a low chuckle. "What happened was not the result of depression."

"Regardless," Spence reached to his side; the bodyguard and Bingham tensed, but Spence had a feeling it was just for show, to let the boss know they were paying attention. Of course, if Spence had actually made a move the brain-dead yokel would never have seen it. He would just roll on the floor wondering how he ended up with a crushed trachea.

Tempting as that was, he instead pulled up the small briefcase and pushed it across the table. "The target is dead, it cannot be traced back to you. The objective is complete. But given that I did not complete the contract, I will return the final portion of the money." He slid the briefcase over.

"Well that's awfully white of you," The old man said, then sucked his bottom lip, pretending to consider. "Unfortunately, things are not so simple."

"Oh, but they are," Spence said, "I told you before that I dictate the terms of my contracts."

"The situation has become more complicated, and it has done so due to your negligence. I am holding you responsible and I expect you to make it right."

"I expect to one day be married to Mila Kunis. Regardless, I will not be staying in San Rita."

Bingham growled something, but the old man just laughed, "What? That bit of business you pulled downtown last night while you were 'looking for the target'?" He gave the last part of the sentence a derisive twist. "That get you nervous?"

Spence froze, for the first time he was genuinely caught off-guard. "What are you talking about?" he asked.

The old man laughed again. "Son, if there's one thing a hometown boy can do it's spot the work of an outsider. I don't see why it should be such a problem, though," his voice suddenly cajoling, "bright boy like you should be able to stay out of the spotlight long enough to get some work done."

"I don't take unnecessary risks." Spence said.

"You'll be taking this one."

Spence sighed, "I'm tired of this. I made my position clear and if you press this issue I will have no compunction about taking laughing boy's Glock and shoving it up his ass before I blow off your lower jaw, and shove a steak knife in that one's," he pointed at Bingham without looking at him, "Carotid artery. I'd be past Santa Maria before the first cop shows up."

The man sucked his bottom lip, "You very well could do that," he allowed, "but you miscalculate. You see, that boy," he nodded to the teen across the aisle, who had drawn a .38 and now had it pointed at Spence, "is my nephew. The people who own this diner? I put up the money that let them keep their house when the bank foreclosed. I have riflemen at the back and front. And if anyone of those four men, or Bingham, or laughing boy, should happen to kill you, I will have an Airstream trailer full of witnesses who just couldn't wait to testify that you got popped robbing the place." He paused to make sure that Spence had taken it in, "It's a small town, son, and they all support the team. Make no mistake, I didn't hire you because I have any shortage of dangerous men."

Spence did some quick calculations in his head. If the old man was bluffing he was hiding it very well, and based on Jr. over there Spence didn't think Pike was.

The uneasy silence was broken by the sound of leather on Formica as the old man passed the briefcase back to Spence. "I don't suggest that you won't be compensated for your efforts," the old man said, gently, as if trying to mend a bruised ego. "You'll get another bonus when the job is completed."

Spence took one last glance at the kid. He pictured him with a hole in his forehead, brains leaking out the back of his head onto the diner wall, a surprised expression on his face. The kid smiled at him. Spence smiled back.

"What's the proposition?" he asked.

He listened. He didn't like what he heard, but he didn't see any way out of it, either. For now. No reason not to bide his time, see how hard the job would be, how quickly he might be able to blow through it and get out of town. Finally, he nodded, the waitress brought out the linguiça and eggs, which the old man smothered in Tapitio and then devoured. He stood up; they shook hands, as though they had discussed nothing more intense than the 49ers' chances that year. Somehow Spence managed to keep the snarl off his face when the old man slapped him on the back.

~ ~ ~

"Shit," Scott said, and pressed the off button on his cell phone with the air of a man who desperately wished he had a receiver to slam.

"What?" Sunny asked. They were sitting in the living room of his condo. It was the typical sitting room for the young and reasonably well-to-do. Flatscreen TV the size of a freeway sign in one corner, next to which were piled a few gaming consoles and a stack of DVDs. Framed one-sheets over the couch, *Grindhouse* and *Moulin Rouge*. The second made Scott assume there was a woman living in the house, but he thought it safer not to ask. They'd come back right after lunch at the Establishment and had been spitballing theories to pass the time, until they could get some real information. Which Scott had just failed to do.

"I just talked to Russell," he grumbled, "They've identified the body, but the police are withholding the information until they can notify the next of kin. Which they'll most likely get around to sometime next spring. This is a bullshit smokescreen if I've seen one."

Sunny shrugged, "Maybe it's just some desk cops in a holding pattern before they can get some clearance from the higher ups."

Scott shook his head, "That's the funny part," he said with a frown, "Russell said that word came from Lieutenant Quinn himself."

"The one who was there last night? I thought he was your buddy."

Scott shook his head, "I don't know if Lieutenant Quinn is anyone's buddy, but he's pretty press-friendly as cops go. He likes having the newspaper on the side of the police and usually gives us just about anything he can, within reason. If he's squashing information, there's gotta be something behind it."

A silence settled over the room. Scott began pacing back and forth. Sunny leaned back in his seat, hands cradling his head, and looked up at the ceiling. Suddenly, he sat up. "San Rita PD doesn't have its own morgue does it? Too small, right?" Scott nodded. "So they go where?" Sunny continued, "County?"

"That's right," Scott confirmed.

Sunny stood up and pulled out his own phone. "Hold on," he said, and dialed a quick number.

"Who are you calling?" Scott asked.

"A source," Sunny replied.

Scott smiled, "Kid, if you think you've got better sources than mine afte-" But Sunny cut him off with a wave of his hand when whoever he was calling picked up.

"Hello, could you connect me with" he muffled his voice slightly at this point, but Scott was able to make out something that sounded like Blazejowski. There was a brief pause. "Morgue," he said. Scott leaned forward. He opened his mouth to ask something, but Sunny held up his finger. There were another few moments of silence, then Sunny started to talk again.

"Heya Bill, how's things," Sunny nodded unconsciously for a moment, then interrupted, "Bill, I'm not going to lie, I'm going to have to catch up with you some other time. Right now I need some information. The name of one of your tenants, he came in last night, was a John Doe until very recently." He paused again. "No, I didn't give my name when I asked for you, how long have we been doing this?" Another pause. "Well, how many John Does do you have that came in in the last day." Another break. "That many? Wow."

Scott could faintly hear what sounded like a list of bullet points coming from the other end. "Well, he's not the car wreck." Sunny interjected. "Not homeless, either. Trust me, Bill, you would have known this one. He would have been messy."

Finally, Sunny started to nod and smile. "That's the one." Another impatient pause, and finally Sunny broke in: "Bill, when has it ever gotten back to you? ... That's what I thought." He quickly strode to the refrigerator where a pen attached to a magnetized notepad hung. He scribbled something down. "Thanks, Bill, you're a peach," he said, "I'll see you at cards."

He hung up the phone and held up the memo pad to Scott, a triumphant smile on his face. He marched over and passed the pad like a boy handing over a report card. If Sunny wasn't mistaken, Scott was working to suppress a look that was damn close to admiration.

"Name mean anything to you?" Sunny asked casually. Scott looked down at the blue notepad. The name read "Harper Lewis."

Scott stood up and shrugged on his overcoat and gave a small smile. "I'll have to check my sources."

~ ~ ~

Karl Winslow was a townie and saw no reason to deny it.

He wore flannel shirts, a large belt buckle and his high school ring, all without irony. He drank Silver Bullet tallboys and smoked Marlboro Reds. He worked hard landscaping and painting houses with his old man, spent three or four nights out of the week at the bar, and no matter how drunk he was Saturday, he always made it to church on Sunday – so long as it wasn't football season.

He talked about as quickly as the average tree, but that didn't mean he was slow. He had dark auburn hair, deeply hooded eyes and a well-toned, rangy physique, which all helped him get more puss than a litter box, though he wasn't one to talk. He was slow to anger and didn't start many fights, though he always finished them. He liked beer and weed and he didn't say no to a line or a bump now and then, though he did that rarely enough that it actually qualified as an indulgence, one that a tour in Iraq and half a round in The Gan had earned him. He was careful though to keep clear of meth, and that included meth heads and meth dealers.

A couple of cops knew him by name, including a few he'd graduated with in high school, much to his distress. But he'd never been in any real trouble outside of Afghanistan, and had nothing on his record.

He was outside The Horns, watching the Thursday night traffic go by. Townie girls in their summer clothes, with their bleached blonde hair, drinker's pooches and fat asses, college girls dressed up in skintight pants and revealing blouses, decked out and made up like they were on the runway and not the bar scene of a small city no one gave much of a shit about. The jukebox changed from Johnny Cash to Journey and the folks inside gave a cheer. Karl rolled his eyes and wondered about the company he kept.

He and some friends were at the bar helping one of their own celebrate closing the deal on his house. They had all been on the football team together. Now they worked in the oil fields, or as movers or air conditioner repairmen. The house his friend had bought was outside the San Rita city limits, in the Shit Cities, a place upon which the newly minted homeowner once spewed as much bile as he could muster. There would be plenty of time to bust his balls about that later, but tonight was a night for celebration. Besides, not many workingmen could afford a house in San Rita any more. Still, it seemed odd, and a little sad to Karl, that this generation of San Rita Lions would be raising boys who would end up playing for the City Greyhounds. It was as though something he couldn't quite put into words was passing before his eyes.

The cops were out in full force that night. The bike cops flitting about like locusts, parting the crowds at their whim. Those fucking Prowlers, with engines like muscle cars from a seventies movie trolling up and down the main drag, the sound drowning out the club music from the inside. Trying to intimidate with a sheer show of money, as though they spent their days battling gang bangers and snipers instead of rousting homeless people and drunks, with time for the occasional B&E or possession bust. Gotta have the muscle of a Prowler to deal with the likes of those. Cops like these would never know what action really meant.

Karl shook his head and went back inside. He had tipped his seat against the bar to mark it for him. He had ordered no drink but found a fresh tallboy waiting for him. He sat down and caught Heather's eye; the bartender wore a Ride the Lightning T-shirt cut low. The shirt earned her more tips than the low cut. He held out a couple of singles; Heather shook her head and jerked to her right, which was how Karl turned and found himself looking into the smiling face of Colin McNamara.

He raised his drink to Colin and then took a long pull. "Cheap bastard," he said when he had finished. "Least you could do was spring for something draft."

"Eh," Colin said, with an exaggerated shrug; he was sipping on a Heineken that Karl would swear was covered with a fine layer of dust. "I know you're a man of simple tastes."

Karl grinned and meditated on the pleasant image of his fist flying into Colin's mouth, sending his teeth flying down his throat and mashing his lips to bloody pulp. But only idly. Colin wasn't what you would call a friend, but he and Karl had history together, the kind of history that effortlessly accrued between two people when they grow up alongside one another in the same community. He may not like Colin – and he certainly didn't trust him, the little bastard was an operator – but he was familiar enough to be entitled to a crack without incurring some bodily harm.

But only just.

As if sensing that it might behoove him to remind Karl of their shared history, Colin said, "You're the second person from the old class I've seen today."

"Yeah?" Karl asked without much interest, "Who else?"

"Good ole Amanda."

Karl couldn't help but smile. "Aw yeah? How's she doing?"

Colin shrugged. "She's still the golden girl." Then he reached into his pocket, pulled out a newspaper clipping and got down to business. He pushed the clipping across the bar to Karl. "Seen this guy?" he asked.

Karl squinted in the dim bar light, looking at the newsprint illustration that Colin had pushed in front of him. It was a dull face, round and smooth, the hair pulling back at the temples but not yet graying. The man could have been anywhere from thirty to fifty, his face unlined, his nose a small slash across his face, his mouth a thin stroke. He looked like a bank examiner who would tell you it was nothing personal when he took your house, or an insurance adjuster who would turn down your claim, or a high school math teacher who failed the jocks on purpose. He was so bland and nondescript that Karl was sure he would stick out vividly in his mind if he had seen him. He hadn't.

He shook his head, and Colin gave a quiet curse. "Who is he?" Karl asked.

Colin grumbled, "Supposedly he's the guy who roughed up that college kid last night. I'm beginning to think his friends were too drunk to give an accurate description. I might as well be walking around with a picture of Michael Myers for all the good it's doing me."

Karl gave a low whistle that to Colin sounded pretty damn close to genuine respect, "That guy?" he asked. "He looks like he's the one who should have gotten rolled."

Colin snorted, "Kid did more than get rolled. His skull has a dent the size of a golf divot in it, and if he ever wakes up the best he can hope for is a serious speech impediment and a job pushing a broom somewhere. The parents of Mr. Formerly Bright Future don't much care for that scenario." He killed the rest of the Heineken and then tossed the bottle in the recycle bin behind the bar. He stood up, slapped Karl on the back, and laid down a fiver. "Well, if that's the case, I've got a long night ahead of me still. Someone has to know where this joker was drinking last night. Next round is on me. If on the off chance he's dumb enough to show his face down here, do me a favor and call me first." Karl tipped his tallboy in salute as Colin walked out the front door. As he watched him go, Karl couldn't help but wistfully think how nice it'd be if one day someone came along to beat the cocky out of him.

~ ~ ~

Karl finished the drink he bought with Colin's fiver and made his way outside. He had about eight beers sloshing around inside him now, and he was feeling nicely mellow. He contemplated going home and making an early night of it as he struggled to light his cigarette. It was either go home and smoke a little of the green he'd picked up earlier that day, or stay out and try to score a little tail when the standards got lowered as the night came to a close. Karl was not sure which prospect was more appealing to him at the moment.

He struck at the wheel of his lighter with increasing frustration. The Bic was low on gas and it was tough to get a decent flame going. Suddenly, a sturdy Zippo flame came to his aid. He inhaled gratefully and looked up to thank his savior. He found himself looking into the eyes of Scott Molina. "How you doing, Karl?" he asked.

"Not bad, Mr. Molina," he said, trying to keep the slur out of his voice as much as possible. Though he knew that Molina had one hell of a bent elbow himself, he couldn't help it. He had known Scott since childhood. He had been one of the procession of middle-aged men with beer on their breath who had served as his father's friends at football games and barbecues of his childhood. After Karl's mother had passed, Karl Winslow the elder had grown less and less social, and the parade had stopped. But Scott Molina would always retain for Karl the effortless authority of one who had literally looked down on him when he was young. Seeing him show up at his watering hole made him uncomfortable. "What brings you out on the town tonight?"

"I'm looking for someone," Scott said. "Guy about your age named Harper Lewis. You know him?"

Karl couldn't suppress a drunken chuckle, "Whadda I look like, a directory?" Scott frowned at him with a severity that caused Karl to snap back into dutiful mode. "I'm sorry, it's just that that's the second time in an hour someone's come to me looking for someone down here. I guess I really am spending too much time at the bars, eh?"

Scott's frown deepened. "Someone came by tonight looking for Harper Lewis?"

Karl waved his hand, "No someone else looking for someone else, it's unrelated. Sorry." The last part came out in a jumble. Karl took a long drag on his cigarette to right himself, "Sure, I know Harp. Well, I mean, I don't *know* him. I wouldn't call the guy a friend, but I know who he is."

"More of an acquaintance?" Scott asked.

Karl shook his head. "Just a guy I know from around the way. Never had a reason to get friendly with him. Never wanted one."

"Why? Bad reputation?" Scott asked.

Karl shrugged, "Nothing concrete, but he's one of Pike's rough boys, and if you're just a little ole townie like me it's best to give them a wide berth."

Scott nodded as though this were sage counsel. Karl continued wondering how much he was going to regret saying when he sobered up the next morning, but what the fuck, when you were going to hell might as well take the free handbasket.

"Truth be told, word around the campfire is that Pike isn't the only one that Lewis has been serving." He glanced around; there was no one for twenty yards and the music from the bar – The Boss this time, singing his song about the darkness at the edge of town – "Word is he's been talking to San Rita PD. Story goes that a couple of tweakers sought old Harp out as a silent partner. You know, 'Give us a couple hundred dollars for some Sudafed and propane and we'll turn it into a couple thousand.' When really what they mean is 'Give us a couple of hundred so we can get high for two weeks.' Typical tweaker burn. Well, the next thing you know, San Rita PD raids the squat those two tweakers are cooking at. And

Lieutenant Quinn gets to pose on the front of the paper and show how proactive he is about the meth menace."

Scott froze, his own cigarette stopped in the air halfway to his lips. Karl had seen hunting dogs go less tense. After a moment he finally spoke. "Are you telling me," he asked, voice quavering with coiled energy, "That Mark Quinn knew Harper Lewis?"

"Knew him?" Karl scoffed. "Man they're probably going to announce their engagement any day, I swear." He stopped, his alcohol-sodden synapses had begun to fire, "Wait, why did you say 'knew'?" he asked.

Scott stared at him. "I always liked you best out of all my friend's kids because you were the only one who knew how to keep quiet. That still true?"

Karl paused for a moment then nodded, "Yes sir."

Scott clapped him on the shoulder; it didn't sting the way it did with Colin, "Good man." He murmured. He looked the slightly weaving Karl up and down. "You need a ride?" he asked.

"Nah," Karl sniffed. "I'm walking home."

Scott slipped a twenty into his front pocket. "Take a cab ride on me." Then he turned and left, with the air of a man with a definite destination. Karl decided to have another round before he left. He would still have enough left over for the taxi afterward.

~ ~ ~

Scott looked over at Sunny, who was gazing out the passenger window like a kid as they drove. Scott just couldn't quite get a bead on the guy. He felt like he was simultaneously underestimating him and expecting too much. Truth be told, he wasn't sure why he was even bringing Sunny out with him, except, well, he had been there when it had started, so he might as well be there when things presumably ended.

He had knocked on Sunny's door just before eleven. He still hadn't gotten the kid's number. The woman he had figured lived there from his earlier visit had answered. She was naturally pretty, even without makeup and dressed in a baggy pair of sweats and a baggier Ramones T-shirt – perhaps especially when dressed like that. She was young – Scott would put her under twenty-five – and her hair was dyed an alarming shade of red just shy of stop-sign intensity. She had introduced herself as Alicia, invited him in and offered him a cup of tea that Scott had declined.

Scott claimed he needed Sunny's help with a story the two of them had been working on. Alicia called out to him and a bemused Sunny came downstairs. Scott gave the same barebones explanation he had given to Alicia. Sunny smiled apologetically to her gave, a quick kiss, and then the two were off into the night.

Scott filled Sunny in on the details he had uncovered about the connection between Harper and Quinn. After his story was over, an uncomfortable silence filled the car.

"What?" Scott finally asked.

"I don't like lying to my girlfriend." He turned to Scott. "And I like you lying to her even less."

"Who's lying?" Scott asked, "I told her I needed your help checking out a story, that's exactly what we're doing. Look, man, if you don't want me to come along ..."

"I didn't say that." Sunny said. They were silent again.

"Why are we even going to see Quinn? Shouldn't we be checking out this Pike connection your source talked about? Seems like we're going after the small fish."

"You don't just go to see Pike," Scott said.

"Why, what makes him so special?" Sunny asked. "He's just the local gentry, right?"

Sunny racked his brains for what he knew about Pike. He was Old San Rita, he owned a couple ranches and vineyards, had stock in several of the stores downtown, but Sunny had never heard of him being worse than any of the other local movers and shakers. A few greased palms, the usual suspicions of illegal labor. The only story that stuck out was the time that Pike had footed the bill for a children's park and soccer fields, and then run a four-lane highway straight through it to an industrial park he owned. Turned out, under the former zoning ordinance a road of that size wasn't allowed. Turn the agricultural land into a park, though, and there was no problem. Now semis chugged along the four lanes day and night, pumping a steady cloud of exhaust over the area. A few other things like that.

Scott was quiet for a moment. "There's never anything definite about Pike," he said slowly, "Just a lot of rumors. But I do know that he employs his muscle for more than punching cattle, and I do know that things tend to fall his way at a frequency that suggests more than just luck. At the very least he has an awful lot of pull in this town, and you don't just go up to a man like that's doorbell and accuse him of complicity in another man's death. Not if you don't have something to back it up. And especially not if he might have no compunction about something similar happening to you."

"You're talking about him like he's Tony Montana," Sunny said. "I thought this guy was just another hick with barely enough juice to keep him relative in local politics."

Scott was silent for a moment; "There should be a copy of The Telegraph there on the floor."

Sunny reached down past several empty fast food bags and picked up a yellowed copy of The Telegraph from earlier in the week.

"Front Page, second banner headline," Scott said, without bothering to glance at the paper, groundbreaking on new housing development. "Pike owns the land, the REITS that will be financing the building and the construction company that's building it. A2," he said, without pausing – Sunny flipped the paper open. "City Council meeting, redistricting said agricultural land for residential growth. Five out of those seven seats belong to Pike. Which way did the vote split again?"

Sunny looked down at the article – a neat 5-2 split. "A4, school board meeting, also staffed by people who got there with Pike's money. A7, new shop opening financed by Pike's capital. A10, community calendar, fundraiser for police and firefighters – any guess who'll be the top donor?"

"OK," Sunny said, "I get it."

"He's dug himself into every place in the social strata he could manage. Any bit of influence he could buy, he's purchased. He might not always use it, but he always has the option to."

"OK," Sunny conceded. "But I guess going to see Quinn doesn't seem much safer," Sunny said.

That took Scott aback. He was silent for a moment. "I know the man," he said, wishing he sounded more certain than he did.

They were driving past the country club estates on the outskirts of town, into the area that was known as The Old Country Club, despite the fact that there was no longer any actual country club present in the neighborhood. It had been torn down and split into lots long ago. The houses and lots were just as big, but unlike the new Country Club, there was no guard post, no cameras to take footage of passing license plates – two facts that Scott was suddenly glad of.

Upon reflection, the place was just a little too nice to afford on a cop's salary. But Scott had never thought of Quinn as dirty. It still didn't all fit together for him. Sure, Quinn was trying to cover up that he knew the late Harper Lewis, trying to keep his death quiet as possible – but why? There was no reason a player as low-level as Harper, a mere enforcer at best, if Karl was right, could afford to put an officer with a desk on the take even if he wanted to. He supposed Pike could be behind the whole thing, but that didn't scan either. For one thing, a man like Pike wouldn't have much need to buy influence at a rank as low as Lieutenant. Even if he did, Pike would use a bagman a lot more subtle than Harper and with a lot more distance from himself as well.

They pulled in front of Quinn's house; his truck was in the driveway. Scott turned to Sunny. "Why don't I go in there alone at first?"

Sunny looked confused. "What? Why?"

"He knows me, maybe if I approach him like this he won't feel so threatened. We can find out what's really going on without him shutting down on us."

Sunny looked bewildered. "Why did you even bring me along then?"

"In case I need backup," Scott said.

"You don't think he'll-" Sunny began.

"I don't know what he'll do," Scott said, cutting him off, "The Quinn I know wouldn't. Then again, the Quinn I thought I know wouldn't cover up a death or take bribes from old man Pike either. So I guess my pattern of predicting Quinn's behavior is pretty much shit."

It came out surprisingly bitter, and Scott was surprised to feel a sting in his chest when he said the words. He wasn't close to Quinn, so why did this carry with it the feeling of betrayal? He took a deep breath and calmed himself, and when he spoke again his voice was level.

"All I know is that I'm about to walk into a house with an armed man and accuse him of obstructing the investigation of a wrongful death at the very least. Nobody knows what anyone will do when they are cornered. I sure as fuck don't. I need someone reliable to watch my back, and right now that's you." He turned to Sunny, their eyes locked for a moment, then Sunny nodded. "Thank you," Scott said.

He started to get out of the car. "Wait," Sunny said, "What can I help you with? I mean if you need it." Scott nodded to the back, Sunny turned and saw a wooden baseball bat lying across the floor of the backseat. "You're kidding me," Sunny said. Scott shrugged and started towards Quinn's home.

~ ~ ~

Scott knocked on Quinn's door, heard a groan and then a shuffling sound across the hall. The door opened and a red-eyed Quinn appeared in the doorway. He was still dressed in his work clothes: white linen shirt and black Dickies, red tie undone but still hanging around his neck. Neither of his hands was visible, but Scott had the uncanny feeling that there was a gun in one of them. Whoever Quinn was expecting, Scott was not it. He blinked in bewilderment before finally righting himself. "Scott," he said. There was half a question mark at the end of the statement.

"Lieutenant," Scott said, "I remembered some details about what happened at the paper last night. I thought maybe you'd wanna talk about them."

Quinn's bloodshot eyes narrowed. "And it couldn't wait until morning?"

Scott shrugged. "It could, but you know me, I'm a night owl. I figured maybe we'd have a drink over it."

Quinn ran one hand over his mouth and his other arm shifted; Scott figured the gun was being tucked into the back of his pants. "Sure," he finally said, "Come on in." He turned; sure enough, there was a bulge where his shirt covered his waistband. Scott followed him inside. The door closed behind them; Scott managed not to flinch at the sound.

They went into his kitchen. Quinn was a bachelor, but a tidy one. The stainless steel refrigerator gleamed, as did the white of the sink and the surface of an island above which hung an array of brass pots and pans. A bottle of Jim Beam Black lay on the island, as did a glass full of half-melted ice. That explained the red in his eyes, at least. Quinn was fishing around in a cabinet and brought out a second tumbler. "Ice?" he asked. Scott nodded. Quinn opened the freezer and poured Scott a generous three fingers and an equal portion for himself. Scott nodded his thanks, Quinn held up his glass. "Cheers," Scott said, their glasses touched. The both of them drank.

Quinn's glass hit the counter. "So, what did you remember?"

Scott took another sip, and set his drink down as well. "I remember," he hesitated, but only for a moment, "That you and Harper Lewis knew each other. That he worked for you as a C.I. That you recognized it was his truck and knew it was him from the very beginning. That you chose not to share this information and personally kept his identity from getting out." He took a moment, considered and then let the final blow fall, "And I know that the both of you are in the pocket of Pike." He picked up his drink and took another sip.

Quinn's face looked enraged. "What the hell did you just say?"

"Save it, Mark," Scott said. "Did you hear any sirens? I haven't told anyone yet, I don't have a recorder on. This is just me asking you why. Give me a good enough answer I'll walk right out that door and won't see you again till next time at McCarthey's. That work for you?"

Quinn held his stare for a moment longer, eyes smoldering with anger. Then, like a switch had been flipped, it all went out of him. He hung his head; he looked exhausted. "Fine," he said, with a disgusted shake of the head. "Fine. I knew the kid. I tried to keep it quiet at first because Old Man Pike doesn't like the names of people who work for him in the papers. And then ..." he trailed off, looking away.

Something flashed in Scott's mind, a memory buried, Quinn standing beside the truck, a manila envelope by his side. It hadn't been there before. Had it? "You found something," he said slowly, piecing it together as he spoke. "You found the reason Harper killed himself and it implicates Pike. You were holding onto it for him at first, and now you're trying to use it against him." Quinn met his eyes again; he didn't deny anything. "What was it?" Scott asked. "His suicide note?"

Quinn laughed. "It's way more than a fucking suicide note." His eyes drifted across the room, Scott followed his gaze. On the coffee table in the adjoining living room, just before the big glass patio doors, there lay a blank DVD in the jewel case. Quinn saw Scott follow his gaze, and gave a drunken grin, "I'm going to bury him with that. But first I'm going to take his money."

"Can I see it?" Scott asked. Quinn shook his head.

"You don't want to."

"What's on it?" Scott asked.

Again Quinn shook his head. "You wouldn't be able to keep your mouth shut."

"You know I'm a tight-lipped man."

"Not about this."

Scott looked back over to the disc. Quinn cleared his throat, and when he looked back Quinn had his police revolver pointed at him.

Scott held up his hands. "There's no need for this," he said.

"I'm truly sorry, but there is." Quinn said. His face did look truly sorry, but it was the drunk's remorse that Scott knew from experience came on easy and dissipated quickly. "I can't go up against a man like Pike worrying about loose ends. I have to keep my focus."

"What's Pike got besides a few roughhouse boys?" Scott asked. "Since when can't you handle an old man?"

"You underestimate him!" Quinn cried, the slur in his voice deepening as emotion filled it. "Everybody fucking underestimates him, hell I underestimated him. That's how he wins. They see him with that fucking folksy accent telling his stories, passing out checks, greasing the wheels and slapping backs. They all know he's crooked but they figure the worst of it is the occasional shady real estate buy, maybe fixing a price every once in a while or holding onto some of Uncle Sam's dough. Hell, they admire him for it, treat him like he's a fucking folk hero every time he gets around a zoning restriction. The crafty old fox. He ain't like that, Scott. He is an evil fucking man."

"Then let me help you. We'll bust him together. We give Russell a call and we can have whatever is on that disc in front of the whole county by tomorrow." Quinn laughed at that.

"Who is it you think you work for?" he asked. The question gave Scott pause. He began to back up towards the living room, closer to the door. Aiden circled around the island, cutting him off at the threshold, gun pointed at the middle of his chest. "For what it's worth-" was all he got out before an exit wound the size of a peach obliterated half his forehead. There was the sound of breaking glass. Quinn's brains splattered on the stainless steel refrigerator and landed in the gleaming porcelain sink. Shards of his skull clattered on the Spanish tile. He gave a sound that was not quite a scream and collapsed, limbs flailing as a wild series of electrical pulses hit them.

Old instinct made Scott drop to the ground the second he saw what happened to Quinn. Familiar scents accosted his nose: the smell of blood, the smell of shit. He forced the frenzied receptors of his brain to shut up while he tried to understand what was going on.

The sound of breaking glass centered him. Fact: The shot had come from the patio. Fact: The shooter was coming in through the patio door. Fact: The shooter had a silenced weapon. Fact: There was no way Sunny could have heard the shot. Fact: There were currently several hundred pounds of marble and wood between the shooter and Scott. Fact: This probably wouldn't be the case for long.

He had only one chance.

Keeping low, on all fours, Scott scurried around the corner of the island to where Quinn lay. His flailing arm had tossed the gun midway between Quinn's body and the island. Scott made a break for it, not looking up, knowing that if he looked up he would be lost.

His only salvation was that the shooter had apparently not been prepared for Scott to break cover. He could hear the man's footfalls on the carpet stop as his fingers curled around the metal of the gun's grip. Quinn had turned off the safety; it was a miracle the gun had not gone off when he'd dropped it. Without taking time to aim, Scott rested his elbows on the hard tile floor and took a shot in the direction of the living room.

The gun gave a resounding crack as the shot went wild. Scott finally looked up. He saw the man for just a second as he dove for cover. He was dressed in black with a black knit cap covering his head. His face was open and round and the eyes reflected nothing back at Scott as he ducked out of sight. No fear, no hate – the eyes had no opinion on the matter. The bullet had come nowhere near him; that was all right, it hadn't been what the shot was for.

Scott took a second shot; it went even wilder than the first, burying itself in the ceiling. A rain of plaster fell upon him, turning his hair and face a fine chalky white. There could be no mistaking the sounds for what they were now. He could only hope Sunny was brave enough to save his life.

Scott pushed himself back behind the island and leaned against the wooden drawers in a crouch. He looked down and counted his shots. Four left. Would that be enough? He hadn't fired a gun in a long time, and his aim had never been the best. In a close-range shootout with a professional, he wouldn't stand a chance.

The shooter seemed to realize this at the same time. There was a short "pfft" Like the sound of an air rifle, and the overhead light in the living room went out, the sound of glass breaking louder than the shot. Another "pfft," and the overhead fluorescents in the kitchen went in a shower of sparks. It was dark now.

He heard the footfalls of the man still on the carpet moving quickly. But he thought he heard something else as well, the sound of a door quietly opening and closing. Just wishful thinking? The desperate hope of a man who was about to die? But no, now he thought he heard a second pair of footsteps, and if he did, the killer would notice them as well. He stood up and fired two wild shots away from the door, hoping that would distract the killer for long enough.

It did. The killer fell into a crouch. He was only feet away; he had covered the ground so quickly. He brought up his gun as the last shot echoed out, aiming for Scott's center mass. Scott flinched and wondered if he had just made the last mistake of his life.

That was when Sunny Wan hit the killer with the bat. The man made a sound like "Oomphooo-" as he collapsed. Sunny's swing had been a little low. He had presumably been aiming for the head, but hit him in upper back, right below the neck. The gun flew from his hand and skittered across the tile floor. The killer went sprawling forward and crashed into the island. His arms were out and the full weight of his fall hit his ribs. The crash drove all the air from the man's lungs he bounced off the island and landed on the floor.

The man was on his hands and knees now; Sunny hit him again. Not wide across the back but in the side, connecting with his ribs. There was a resounding crack and the man cried out in pain. He rolled away, towards the living room, not even bothering to go for the gun. Sunny brought down the bat again and missed; shards of tile flew up from the force of the blow. The man was on his feet now in a crouch, clutching his side but moving fast towards the patio door, to once again disappear into the night. He stopped only for a second, Scott saw what he was doing, but it was too late to stop him. The disc on the table disappeared somewhere into his jacket. "Stop! Scott cried, feeling stupid as he said it. But the man was already gone – visible for one moment on the patio as a silhouette, black on black, then vanished into the night.

Scott stared at Sunny, both of them stunned. "Thanks," Scott finally managed to mutter. Sunny could only breathlessly nod. "You touch anything?" Scott asked. Sunny shook his head. Scott took Quinn's revolver, wiped it on his shirt and placed it in his hand. "Come on." He said.

Sunny shook his head in disbelief. "That's not going to fool even the dumbest cop," he said.

"I know," Scott admitted, "But let's not make it easy for them." He wiped off the tumbler he had been drinking from and then put it in the cupboard near the back.

"Why aren't we waiting for the cops?" Sunny asked.

"You were right, Quinn was way crooked. And if he was, anyone can be. They'll either try to pin it on us, or put us within easy range of whoever just ran off." He paused for a second as he glanced around, looking for anything else he might have touched. "And even if they weren't, would you want to try and explain this to them?" He started for the door, Sunny followed. He wiped the door handle and then they walked the block to where the car had been parked.

They hadn't quite cleared the neighborhood when they heard the sirens. "Shit," Scott said. He pulled down a side street, turned off his lights and parked in an empty driveway. For the next five minutes they saw the flashing lights and heard the alarms, as cop cars without number, an ambulance and a fire truck passed by. A few minutes later a patrol car with its lights off passed down the street. Sunny and Scott dropped to the floor. The car continued without stopping. As soon as it cleared the street, Scott started the car and they drove back to Sunny's home.

As they started, Scott filled Sunny in on what Quinn had told him about Pike and the disc the hit man had just made off with. "Probably already shredded by now." Sunny grumbled. Scott couldn't disagree. They drove the rest of the way in silence. When they reached Sunny's home, Scott walked with him to his door. "Shit," Sunny said, "I forgot my keys."

"Think," Scott said. "Did you forget your keys at home? Or did you leave them at the scene?" It came out harsher than he intended.

Sunny craned his head back, closing his eyes in concentration, "No," he said calmly. "No, it's alright, I had them in my hoodie pocket and when I changed into my jacket I left them there." Scott breathed a sigh of relief. Wan bent down to a little ceramic hedgehog that lay in a potted plant by his door. He swung upon the false bottom and removed a key. He went to open his door. Scott grabbed his arm, stopped him. Sunny looked back, surprise and a little anger in his face.

"I know what you kids think of me at the paper." He didn't quite meet Sunny's eyes when he said it, "You think I'm a broken down old man. I am a little broken down at that, I won't deny it." He raised his face to meet Sunny's eyes. "But I don't forget things like what you did back there, and I pay my debts." They stared at each other a moment longer, and then Sunny nodded. Scott let go of his arm and Sunny went back to Alicia's bed.

~ ~ ~

It was another loose end. It seemed as though there had been nothing but loose ends since Spence had arrived in this Godforsaken town. He made it back to his car a half-mile away, hobbling across the golf course, keeping to the shadows. His ribs hurt like a motherfucker, but he couldn't stop to check if they were broken or cracked yet. All he knew was every time he took a breath it felt like he was being kicked in the side with a steel-toed boot.

When he finally reached his car, he took the time to complete a few deep, painful breaths before driving, without his lights, on a complex circuit of country roads that brought him back to San Rita on the opposite side from which he had left it. About five minutes into his half hour drive, when he was reasonably sure he wasn't being pursued, he allowed himself to lose his temper, punching the steering wheel and screaming as loud as his bruised lungs would allow him.

So here were two more people he had to fucking kill. It was all entirely Pike's fucking fault. That smiling old bastard. Pike, who had given him a fucked-up target with fucked-up intel. Pike, who had made Spence feel small and powerless for the first time since he was seventeen years old. Pike, who had blackmailed Spence and then made him kill a fucking policeman in the same town where he was wanted for a violent assault, and it was all because of that fucked-up job that he didn't have time to properly plan for and scout, which he had been forced to wing because of the old man's ridiculous timetable, and now, thanks to that, he had been witnessed in the act for the first time in his professional career.

Spence's ears had turned red; he was burning in a way he had forgotten he knew how to feel. Fuck two more people to kill. He had *three* more people to kill. He didn't care how many brain dead bullnecked nephews and grandkids Pike had on his payroll. Spence didn't care if he had to kill a whole branch of the Pike family tree and half the San Rita graduating class of 2015. He would do it. He'd burn the old man's chicken-shit empire to ashes. He looked over at the disk next to him. So this was what had been so important to Pike? This was what he was willing to murder a cop on his payroll for? Spence had a feeling he had his viewing for the evening planned.

When he arrived at his motel, Spence went straight to his bathroom, where he finally conducted a thorough examination of the damage that had been doled out to him. The ugly yellow beginnings of bruises were forming up along most of his side. He gingerly laid his fingers on his ribs, wincing at the slightest bit of pressure. The ones in the middle of his left side had taken most of the damage, from when that cocksucker hit him when he was on the floor. But when he pressed them with a little more force, enough to make him cry out, they held in place. Spence didn't think they were broken, just cracked. He taped himself up and poured himself a tall tumbler of

Jameson over ice. Then he lay on his bed, opened up his laptop and waited to see what Pike's deep, dark secret was.

Spence did not have any real idea what would be on the video the disc contained. If he were a betting man he would have guessed that it was probably footage of Old Pike with his dick in one of the orifices of a sixteen-year-old San Rita High Cheerleader. Maybe video of Pike receiving money on camera for a briefcase full of hillbilly heroin, or engaged in activity that was likewise unbecoming for such a pillar of the San Rita community.

He was not prepared for what was actually on it. Spence watched the video, then watched it again. There was an expression on his face of genuine shock, a look that rarely visited his features. "Holy shit," he muttered to himself, "You've been a bad bad boy, Pike." By the time he had played the video a third time, he was smiling.

~ ~ ~

Karl really had intended to head home after finishing that last drink. But he was riding high on other people's money and it seemed a shame to waste that kind of momentum. Besides, he didn't have to work tomorrow, and a few more of the old boys from the football team had wandered in, and before he knew it the bartenders were shouting for last call. As he reached into his wallet to square up his tab, Karl felt a heavy hand rest on his shoulder for the third time that night. He turned around to see the bearded face of Bingham Earle peering down on him.

"Why don't we wait awhile?" he asked. "That way we can have a chat when things get quieter? I have a feeling your drinks are on the house anyway." He nodded to the bartender and she placed a cold pint down in front of Karl. Karl nodded his thanks and stifled a gulp.

Bingham was acting friendly, but he always acted friendly. The only reason Bingham usually sought people out was that they were in trouble; he led the shady side of Pike's operations. Karl wracked his brain trying to figure out what he might have been in trouble for. It couldn't be the Molina thing – for one thing the old man was tighter than a drum, for another it was just too soon. So what?

Earle settled his considerable bulk onto the stool next to Karl. Earle had the classic biker's build, a slab of beer muscle in his gut, flanked by big burly arms. He was slightly walleyed and some unfortunate quirk of genetics had left him both hollow-cheeked and double-chinned, which he tried to disguise with a straggly red beard, now streaked with gray. He waited, silently staring ahead, while the bouncers hurried people out the door, and the bartenders suddenly remembered urgent chores that needed to be done in the back room. A few minutes later they were alone in the bar. Only then did Earle speak. "There's an opportunity," he said.

Karl gave an inward sigh of relief. This would be a lot easier than he would have thought. He smiled. "I do appreciate the offer, Mr. Earle."

"Call me Bing," he interrupted.

"But I can't say I'm interested."

"Why not?"

Karl shrugged. "I don't have much ambition in that way. I make good enough money and I stay out of trouble. I see no reason to upend that fairly even keel."

Bing nodded his head sagely, "You say that now, sure, and you're probably right. You've got drinking money, pussy and a warm place to shit. What more does a young man need?" He paused. "But ten years down the line? Five? You'll feel that sting of ambition, but by then it'll be too late. You really want to spend the rest of your life busting your ass in the sun everyday for assholes with more money than you? You don't think that life wears on a man? Hell kid, all you've gotta do is look at your daddy to see what it does to a man." He held up his hands in a no-disrespect gesture. "No offense, kid, we're just talking straight."

The picture of his father, stoop-shouldered, skin the color and texture of jerky, eyes downcast, voice nearly inaudible came unbidden to Karl. That stung. "Seems to me that the job you're offering is nothing but busting my ass for an asshole with more money than me," he said, and gave Bingham his best shit eating-grin as he stared him in the eye, "Like you said, we're just talking straight."

For a moment Bingham's eyes burned; Karl had gone too far and couldn't help but wonder if he was about to disappear. He found he didn't much care, and if the ginger man thought he'd go down easy, he had another thing coming. Haji couldn't kill him, there was no fucking way Bingham Earle would do the job. He pressed on. "While we're on the subject, I will note that I have spent four years of my life institutionalized. I hope not to spend any more of it that way." He held up his hands again. "No matter how unlikely that scenario might be."

That seemed to give Bingham the moment he needed to regain his control, and when he spoke again his voice was smooth. "That may be so, but you just think about it. You're a kid, you only think about the present. You need to look up and see that your life is a long road in front of you. There are a lot of days ahead. Make sure you know how to spend them. What's your phone number?" Karl gave it to him; Bingham wrote it down in a notebook, "I'll be giving you a call in the next couple of days," Bingham said. "Whether you pick up or not is up to you."

He started to get up. "Why me?" Karl asked. Bingham stopped.

"Well, as you noted, you know how to keep out of trouble. You've got a clean record, you don't lose your temper, you don't do a lot of flashy stupid shit. You got ties to the community, and besides," he stopped and smiled. "Pike likes a man who knows how to serve."

~ ~ ~

Only sheer exhaustion allowed Scott to fall asleep after returning from Sunny's house. He woke up barely five hours later, the restlessness that had haunted him for the past two days driving him out of sleep. The sun had not risen yet, but Scott knew sleep was a hopeless proposition. He made himself coffee in the dark.

He had felt this brightness before in his life. This incessant buzz, like an undercurrent just beneath his conscious mind that told him he was hunting. It had rarely led to any place good. Scott thought he had killed it after the last time, but apparently it had just lain dormant. He looked out his window at the first pinkish tinge in the night sky.

He did not know why he should feel this way. The trail had gone cold. He would be very lucky if he was not indicted in the murder of a police officer, he was in the midst of a conspiracy which apparently involved the richest, most powerful man in the city, and the only evidence was in the hands of a professional killer who had probably destroyed it by now. Even if the evidence still existed, God knew what it was.

Yet, it wasn't fear or frustration that Scott felt now, it was something very near elation. As he watched the sun rise he knew, for the first time in thirty years, why he was on the face of the Earth. He had a mission. He had a purpose. He probably wouldn't achieve either; he might die a violent death trying. But he would try. It had been a very long time since Scott had felt much like trying.

As he took his first sip of coffee, a smile crept across his face.

~ ~ ~

A few miles away, Sunny was not taking such a satirical view of the sudden changes his life had gone through. Sunny was not a violent man; he had indeed spent most of his life scrupulously avoiding violence, chaos, confrontation and whatever other kinds of trouble might appear in his placid life.

Yet in the space of twenty-four hours he had watched not one but two men die violently, and he had delivered a savage beating to another. He wasn't an idiot; he knew what he had done had been necessary, that the violence he inflicted had been nothing compared to what the other man would have done to Sunny if he had checked his swing. What bothered him was the savage heat he had felt in the moment, that as he saw the man hit the ground his first instinct had been to bash the fallen enemy in the head until he could see his brains. The presence of such ugly impulses within himself was another thing Sunny had spent a long time trying to avoid.

Worse was the feeling that he was not done yet. He had no idea what he would say to Scott when they saw each other at the paper today, but he knew that if the old man had found another lead, he would follow it, God help him. Sunny felt as though he was in the midst of a dark lake the bottom fathoms below him, the shore nowhere in sight. He could only keep swimming. If he stopped, he'd drown.

The worst part was Alicia though. He couldn't tell her; he had tried at breakfast, but somehow the words, "Well, I got into a fight with a hit man over the corpse of a police officer," wouldn't come out when she asked him how the night had gone. He had simply mumbled "Fine," and endured a puzzled look that he was afraid would break his heart.

He felt as if a wall had risen between them, all the worse because he knew it was of his own making. He knew she sensed it too. He held their relationship, something delicate and wonderful, in his hands, and knew that with just the slightest amount of misapplied pressure he would shred it like tissue.

Lost in these thoughts, he reached the Telegraph in what felt like no time at all. He sat in the parking lot for a few minutes, trying to figure out if he even wanted to go in. The bland industrial architecture looked strangely imposing today, as if there was something terrible waiting for him inside. He had plenty of sick time; he could just turn around right now and try to ride the whole thing out. Hell, Russell had explicitly ordered him to take more time if he needed it. It was tough to think of a situation where he would need it more. Sunny gulped, then opened the car door and started towards the office. He wasn't a coward; he would face what was coming.

Nothing out of the ordinary waited for him at his desk – a few bits off the wire, some press releases from bands coming through town, looking for a little coverage in his column in the weekend entertainment section. All in all, the average pile on his desk. Just an ordinary morning, unaltered by the violence a few hours ago. He started to organize the papers into "things he could actually use and crap, and had almost finished when an all too-familiar-voice broke his concentration.

"Hey," Scott said, as he leaned against the entrance to his cubicle with a mug of coffee in one hand. He looked annoyingly fresh, or at least as fresh as he ever did.

"Hey," Sunny said, then looked back down at his work.

This seemed to catch Scott off-guard; he cleared his throat. "Mind if I look at that paper?" He asked hesitantly, "I wanna see how that Amanda girl did with my beat. You know her?"

Sunny shrugged and passed the paper over to Scott. He really had no feelings one way or the other about

Amanda. He hadn't had much contact with her, but she had a good reputation. Or at least, had not yet developed a bad one, which in a paper as small as San Rita's often amounted to the same thing.

Scott took a sip of his coffee. "So," he said, after another moment proved that Sunny had no intention of starting this conversation. "Any ideas about last night?"

That did it. Sunny checked to make sure was no one eavesdropping, swiveled around in his chair, faced Scott full-on, and looked him in the eye. "Yeah Scott, I've got plenty of ideas, most of them about pretending that last night never happened."

Scott's face fell. "Look, kid, I don't blame you, but you're in this now, you can't just hide under the covers and hope it goes away."

"Oh, but I think I can. You were open with me last night, so let me tell you something about myself. I know people think I'm here because I couldn't hack it in the major markets. Truth is, I turned them down. I like it here. I spent twenty years of my life in big cities and I hated it. I was four years old when the L.A. riots happened and everyone from down south started looking for Korean shops to burn." Well, that answers that, Scott thought. "It left an impression. I like living in a town where I know my car is going to be where I parked it, where my girlfriend has a decent chance of getting home without getting raped, and if I forget to lock my door it's not taken as an invitation to steal my shit. I like being safe, and it's been going pretty well until a couple of days ago, when I fell into your orbit."

Scott's face was stony. "Fine," he said. "But word to the wise, kid: I've worked big cities and I've worked small towns and I've worked places that are worse than either, and let me tell you. Here's no better than there. It's just better at hiding it, is all. It's all human nature. All you have to do is look in the paper. Look here." He had the front page of the local section of the paper and pointed to it. As he looked down to read it he abruptly stopped talking. His face went gray.

"What?" Sunny couldn't keep himself from asking. Scott didn't answer; he was looking down at the paper in a trance. "What?" Wan asked.

Scott shook himself and glared at Sunny, "Nothing," he said as he folded up the paper and tucked it under his side. "Stay here, be safe." He walked out into the hall. Sunny took a deep breath and followed him.

"Hey," he said, Scott kept walking, "Hey!" Sunny said actually loud enough to turn some heads. He caught up with Scott and pulled the paper from under his arm. Scott struggled for a moment but let him have it. Sunny began paging through the paper, trying to find what had caught Scott's eye.

"B1," Scott said impatiently. Sunny glared up at him and went to the section. Staring back at him was the face of the killer from the night before.

The sketch the police artist had provided was ill-defined, but Sunny knew that was because the killer's real face was ill-defined. It was unmistakably him. Sunny's eyes scanned back and forth over the columns; apparently he had put some kid in the hospital the night before last.

"Who the fuck is this guy?" Sunny whispered.

"One way to find out," Scott replied, putting his finger on the byline.

~ ~ ~

For the first time in days Spence felt good. He had two objectives, three targets, and unlike most people Spence was never intimidated by what he had to do. It was only when there was no clear objective that he got anxious. So long as he had workable goals he was happy, even if those workable goals involved killing the most powerful man in town and two men whom he didn't know.

His side ached, but not as much as he had expected it to. The ugly yellow bruises had turned black and purple, but so long as he didn't jab his side unexpectedly and kept his breathing shallow they didn't bother him all that much. He popped some of the emergency codeine he had stored, just to be safe.

He had woken up early to catch the local news report on Quinn's murder. Nothing useful had come out of it – no mention of a third party or witnesses. He had expected that much. He supposed it was possible that the police were simply trying to cover up the existence of his targets, but he found it much more likely that his quarry had just gone to ground. That was all right. This was San Rita, not much ground to go to.

Afterward he had sketched out his plans for Pike. They hadn't taken long. He sent a quick message setting up the time and place for their meeting, then went to the diner across the street from his hotel to have a hearty breakfast.

Linda's was the kind of breakfast place that Spence loved and rarely found outside of L.A. Real Formica and linoleum, with a long countertop that ran parallel to a row of crimson stools. It was devoid of folksy junk, stupid crap on the wall and trendy health scams. He ordered a steak and eggs; the steak came so rare that it turned the eggs red, and the coffee was strong and bitter. It was perfect.

About midway through he glanced at the paper someone had left in the booth. He idly began to page through it, no more than glancing at the stories. All small-town papers were the same, anyway. By the time he reached the high school sports scores his eyes had glazed over, and he turned to the much more productive activity of sopping up the last of his steak juice with his toast. He signaled for the bill and idly wondered if he should catch a movie before going to meet with Pike.

He took a sip of his coffee, rifled past the sports section and reached the last section of the paper – comics, reviews taken off the wire, and a few small-time columns. He opened the paper and nearly spat out the coffee in his mouth; instead, he went into a coughing fit after managing to force it down.

The picture wasn't illustrated the way it would be in a fancy newspaper, just a small color photograph in the top left hand corner of the column, entitled "Wan Way or Another." Staring back at him was a broad-faced kid with a wide smile, one he hadn't been wearing when he had rearranged Spence's ribs last night with a baseball bat. He looked at the byline and started to laugh. The waitress came up to Spence with his change and an expectant look. Spence wiped his eyes. "Sorry," he chuckled. "I just saw something funny in the paper."

He tipped generously.

~ ~ ~

Amanda was not quite prepared to find two of the paper's most seasoned reporters suddenly perched on the entrance to her cubicle, like a couple of strangely genial crows. Though she knew Sunny enough to say hello to him while passing in the halls, she had not shared more than two words with Scott in all her time at the paper, and truthfully he terrified her just a little bit.

He actually did look like a bit like a crow in his black overcoat (which, given that it was just barely under sixty degrees that morning, seemed a bit excessive) and work pants. His long, sharp nose and slightest of stoops gave him a distinctly birdlike posture, and it didn't take much to think of his voice, worn rough by cigarettes and, as office rumor would have it, an alcohol intake that was more than social, as a caw.

If Sunny was a bird, it was more like one drawn by Disney: Pigeon-toed, with the extra twenty pounds of a man in a stable relationship, his usually affable face looked strangely anxious. As her mother would say, something distinctly hinky was going on.

After a few pleasantries Scott started in, with a rhythm to his voice that sounded suspiciously like the patter in the old cop shows and movies Amanda's father loved: "That was a nice job you did with the stories yesterday. Thanks for filling in for me."

"My pleasure," she said, and waited for more.

Scott coughed, filling her cubicle with the scent of burnt tobacco. "That story on B3, the frat boy beating, you going to do a follow-up?"

She shifted in her chair, feeling as though she were being tested. "Not much to follow up on," she said slowly. "Cops don't have any new leads, at least none they feel like sharing. I called the hospital this morning and the kid still hasn't woken up. There's no way to go forward with it that I can see." After a moment, she added. "Why?"

For just a moment Amanda was sure a flash of disappointment had crossed Scott's face. Scott tried to shrug nonchalantly, he didn't do it very well. "No real reason. Just seemed pretty rich, there's a lot there – violence, class conflict, the whole bar controversy again. People like reading about that stuff. Seems like there could be more here." He held up a preemptive appeasing hand. "Not that you didn't do a good job with it. That's why I'm saying this."

Her instincts weren't appeased, "True," she said with a shrug. "But without any new developments there's nothing to hang the story on."

"But there haven't been any new developments," Sunny said.

"That's what I said."

"Right," Scott said, with a smile that looked slightly queasy, "Well, we'll let you get back to it." They turned to leave, and Amanda closed her eyes and made a decision.

"You fellas wouldn't be trying to scoop me, would you?" They both turned simultaneously in a way that looked so practiced that Amanda had to stifle a giggle.

"Noooo," Sunny said, drawing the word out. "We're not trying to scoop you."

"Because it is my story, and even though I haven't been around forever like you guys, I would like to think I'm entitled to a little professional courtesy."

"Look kid," Scott said. "I'm not trying to steal a byline from you. I thought perhaps you could shed some light on an unrelated matter. Turned out to be a bust, there's nothing more to be said."

"I don't think you're being truthful with me." She forced herself to continue in the heat of Scott's glare. "What's the unrelated matter? Maybe I *can* shed some light on it."

"You don't want to know." Scott said.

"Trust him on this," agreed Sunny. "I'd trade places with you if I could." That earned him a glare from Scott.

They turned and started walking again, and Amanda felt the familiar sting of being left out of the boys' club again. Great strides had been made it was true, and yadayadayada, but the male Omertà was still strong at times and it never got any less annoying. Time to play her trump card. "I said the police didn't have any new information, I know someone else who may."

Scott turned gave her an appraising look. "Now it's my turn to say that I don't buy it."

She looked up at him defiantly. "Buy it or not, it's legit." She decided to push a little harder. "And if you're coming to me, it's probably the only lead you've got." The two of them looked at each other, and Amanda couldn't help but feel a little bit satisfied at the helplessness she saw on their faces.

~ ~ ~

A few minutes of intense negotiation later they piled into Amanda's Prius, Scott forced in the backseat and looking about as happy as a wet cat. He tried to light a cigarette in the back, but Amanda shot him the withering glare she had inherited from her mother, and with a loud sigh he tucked it behind his ear.

She wouldn't tell them who they were going to see, or even where they were going, but from her route it soon became obvious that they were heading towards Avalon Beach. The green rolling hills that surrounded the paper soon gave way to surprisingly heavy woods, broken up only by the occasional million-dollar lot with an appropriately palatial estate on it.

It was not as if, once they crested the final rise and came into view of Avalon, things suddenly became slightly more humble. The town had basically been torn down and rebuilt. Nearly all of the developments were new and, none sold below the mid-five-hundred-thousands. It was a stark difference from the Avalon Beach Scott had known when he had first moved to the area. At that time it had been all shacks, fleabag motels and biker bars. Amanda drove through the small downtown and made an abrupt left about five blocks from the beach. They were in a residential area, mostly condos but a few big houses as well. Most of the hotels were at least a few more blocks up. Amanda abruptly stopped the car.

The house they were in front of seemed specifically designed to bring down the property values of those around it. Scott couldn't help but marvel a little bit. It was as though a lot from Avalon Beach circa 1990 had been pushed through a time warp by some prankster God and forcefully inserted into the paradise for genteel retirees they'd been driving through.

The house was small, little more than a shack, and of indeterminate color. Any paint that was on it was peeling, and the porch sagged as though it was under the weight of a party of morbidly obese invisible men in deck chairs. The lawn was a field of dirt with occasional patches of yellowing, dispirited grass.

"Nice place," Sunny deadpanned. Amanda ignored him and started walking, not to the house but around it. Down the long driveway to its right, a garden shed came into view. It was in markedly nicer shape than the house that hid it, well maintained with a fresh coat of paint. The backyard itself was also in better condition than the front would suggest; aside from a few toys and stuffed animals littered about that suggested a very young child, it was dominated by a well-tended vegetable garden. Scott was surprised to see that unlike the front, the back of the house was very well maintained, the paint fresh, the windows clean, the gutters clear – not at all like the derelict face it presented to the world.

Just as they were about to cross from the side yard into the back, a huge Rottweiler came around the corner of the house and deposited itself in their path. The dog didn't bark, it didn't even bother to growl. It merely laid its two hundred pounds across their path and calmly stared up at them with yellow eyes, informing them that this was as far as they got without an invitation, and, should they wish to press the matter, he would be more than willing to accommodate.

Sunny and Scott stopped in their tracks. Amanda kept walking. "It's fine," she said. The dog begged to differ. It got to its feet, still not growling but ignoring her outstretched hand and placating clucks, firmly blocking her way as if to say, "I'm sorry, ma'am but you are no longer on the list." Amanda sighed, and stopped. "Colleen!" she called out. "Will you come out here and call off Zoltan?"

A few moments later the door to the shed opened and a heavy-breasted woman in jeans and a Led Zeppelin T-shirt, carrying a two-year-old child on her hip, opened the door. She looked about the same age as Amanda, though she had that worn look that told Scott you could measure the difference in life experience between the two in decades. She didn't bother to disguise her surprise at seeing Amanda. But she slapped her thigh with the flat of her hand and Zoltan drew back like an electric gate, giving each of them a careful sniff as they walked past.

Colleen chewed gum with the enthusiasm of someone who really wants a cigarette, wintergreen fumes wafting about ten feet in front of her. "What are you doing here?" she asked when Amanda came close, not unfriendly, just trying to establish the facts.

Amanda jerked her head over her shoulder at Sunny and Scott. "They have some information for Colin," she said. Scott was surprised to hear that, but hid it, impressed by how smoothly Amanda delivered the lie. The girl might have real talent. It seemed everyone was playing their cards close to their chest; he saw no reason not to follow suit. Colleen looked over her shoulder at them with appraising eyes. Sunny waved. The child on her hip appraised them just as carefully with strangely solemn eyes. Apparently, they passed initial scrutiny, because she turned back to Amanda and said, "He's on his run, but he should be back within a half hour, you're welcome to wait." She led them into the small garden shed.

~ ~ ~

Colin was by no means what you would call a spiritual man. He had rejected the Catholicism of his childhood and saw no reason to replace it with an equally specious set of guidelines. Across his shoulders were inked the words "Nec Spe Nec Metu" the only creed he cared to keep.

But there were some aspects of religion that he did understand. He suspected that what religious folk got from prayer and meditation was similar to what he received from running. It cleared his mind of the trivial and the day-to-day, focused his thoughts on what was important. The rhythm of it allowed him a kind of clarity that he experienced very rarely in other areas of his life. Usually.

He always ran the same stretch of beach at varying lengths. Avalon Beach had been his home since he was a kid, though it had changed a whole hell of a lot since then – except for his place. A stubborn reminder of the way things were. He smiled to himself. Avalon Beach had been a small blue-collar beach town when he had been growing up, barely big enough to support a few bars, a post office, a convenience store and a rickety pizza place that managed to stay open despite nobody ever having eaten there to Colin's knowledge.

Then an oil pipeline under the beach had burst, and the residents of Avalon found their beachfront property turned into a toxic liability. The pipeline had been built by a construction group owned by old man Pike, so no one was all that surprised when Pike came through offering buyouts to just about everyone in town through a real estate group. Nearly everyone took him up on it.

Everyone but Colin's old man. Colin couldn't claim to like the old son of a bitch. He was a drunk and a self-pitying complainer who had driven his mother all the way across the country with his open hand. But the bastard was stubborn, Colin gave him that. He held out until Pike could postpone no longer. One oil-company-sponsored clean up later and Pike's developers came in and continued their mission to transform as much of the San Rita area into Santa Barbara North as they could manage, which they did with brute efficiency. Property values shot up again and no one could be sure just how much Pike had netted in the deal. The only holdout was Colin's little eyesore.

The old man had died soon after. Colin had not been overly broken up about it. He had his father cremated and scattered his ashes to the four winds. But when one of Pike's men came and offered him $600,000 and then $750,000 dollars for the house, which Colin doubted would appraise at $100,000, he decided to keep the bungalow as a monument of sorts to the old man. A big old middle finger in place of a tombstone. Colin couldn't help but think the old man would have approved.

He was six miles into his eight-mile run, keeping a steady eight-minute pace through beach sand. The beach was mostly empty, the weather just cold enough to keep everyone away but a few dedicated surfers trying to make the most out of some unimpressive chop. Normally, the isolation and endorphins would be enough to send him to at least a slightly elevated plane. Instead he was stuck in the here and now, the sand shifting under his feet sending up little plumes behind him, making the idea of forward progress seem increasingly like a joke.

The fact was he had dick. He had gone to every bar, worked every source he had on both sides of the law, talked with more barflies than he cared to remember, and he still had nothing. Not only did no one know who the attacker was, no one would even cop to seeing him. It was as if the perpetrator had driven into town, said to himself, "Hmm ... I feel like roughing up someone privileged," and then continued on his merry way. There was just nothing to go on.

The only upside was that, according to his sources on the San Rita PD, they didn't have anything to write home about either. He could deal with failure, but getting shown up by that crew of pampered pussies would have added an extra layer of humiliation he just couldn't deal with. Still, the time was quickly coming that if someone didn't solve the case, no one would. It was as cold as the pizza that had been in his fridge for the last three days, and just as appealing.

It wasn't that he felt any real sympathy for the victim of the crime. He had done some checking on the kid, trying to figure out if this might have been a personal beef disguised as a random attack, and while he hadn't found anyone who was mad enough at the kid to hire someone to cave in his skull, the portrait that had emerged was of an entitled, belligerent Tap Out-clad d-bag who would have eventually found someone to put him into a coma. The case was work for hire, nothing personal.

What was personal was the mile-wide competitive streak deeply ingrained in him, and a fierce amount of pride, the two of which had combined like competing storm fronts to create a frustrated energy that was greater than the sum of its sources. He was someone who was good at his job. His job was finding people who other people wanted found, and the fact that this little fucker was eluding him was making it very hard to keep an objective professional distance.

He turned off the beach, running between two sets of swings up a flight of cement steps to the oceanfront stores. The town looked eerily deserted. It was the wrong time of the week in the wrong time of the year. Most of the hotels were near empty. Most of the stores in this part of town relied on tourists for their trade and looked like they could easily be shuttered. A lone hotdog man leaned on his cart looking slightly desperate. Colin would have to go buy a brat for lunch and give him a break if he could remember.

He ran between the shadows of the five-story hotels and three-story condos, walking the last block to his own humble abode in order to cool down. He did a few stretches on the front porch, pounded a protein shake and hopped in the shower. He emerged five minutes later in his back yard, barefoot, wearing Dickies and a wife beater. "Hey, Colleen!" he called. It came out "CAHLEAN." The door to his little office opened and Amanda emerged. Oh shit, Colin thought.

Two men came out with her, flanking her on either side. Colin didn't recognize the Asian one, but the one on her left was Scott Molina. Colin's first, irrational thought was that Amanda had told Scott about the crack he had made about his drinking and he was about to be beaten down by a bunch of fucking reporters in a bizarre gang-like rep restoration. This was unlikely – if Scott had to get revenge on everyone who made jokes about his drinking he'd have time for little else but he couldn't think of any better reason for these people to come knocking on his door.

Somewhat belatedly, he put on a smile and tried to play host. "Hello," he said walking across the backyard, hand extended. He shook hands with Scott and the Asian guy, who he thought introduced himself as Sunny, but he wasn't sure if he had heard right; Amanda kept her arms crossed. "So," he said after the initial round of introductions. "What can I do for you?"

It was Scott who spoke in his sandpaper voice: "Amanda tells us you're working for the family of that boy who was beaten the other night."

Whatever Colin had been expecting, it hadn't been this. "That's right," he said.

"Find anything interesting?" Scott asked.

Colin shrugged, "I'm afraid that's confidential; the family is paying the bills. They get the information first. I tell them news that they already read in the paper, they're not going to think their money is well-spent."

"This isn't about the paper." Scott said.

"Oh?" Colin asked, his eyebrow cocked, "Exactly what is it about?"

Scott and Sunny glanced at each other. For the first time, a real thrill of excitement went up Colin's spine. They had something, all right; Amanda was out of the loop at the moment and they hadn't yet discussed just how much they would tell Colin. If he had been a cop and had access to three locked rooms, he could have had them working against each other in ten minutes flat. But it was just little old him here. He'd have to play this a lot more delicately.

Scott spoke. "We may have information about the attacker that would be helpful to you. That we would be willing to exchange for some of the information you have collected."

"How do I know I need your information?" Colin asked, over a beating heart.

"You don't have him," Sunny responded. "By my reckoning that means any information would be useful information." Colin suppressed a flinch. That had caught him off-guard. B2 and aw shit you struck my battleship. He'd have to watch that kid.

He tried to play it nonchalant. "Maybe so, but I still need to have some idea about what you're offering before I give anything up."

There was another glance between Mutt and Jeff, and then Scott spoke again. "We have good reason to believe that the perpetrator of the crime you're investigating is not only still in town, but has almost certainly participated in another crime."

"What crime?" Colin asked. Scott just shot him a look over his glasses. It was his turn.

Colin hesitated; this was San Rita, it wasn't exactly like he couldn't look at the day's headlines and play "One of These Things Is Not Like the Other." Then again, just because he was pragmatic didn't mean he didn't believe in fair play. Besides, it wasn't like he had much to give.

He shrugged and tried to turn his bullshit into something more substantial. "I've more narrowed down who he's not." Amanda scoffed; Colin ignored her. "He's not local. I've been to every bar in San Rita, no one knows who this guy is. As far as I can tell this kid didn't have any enemies who were pissed enough or powerful enough to hire a professional. My theory is the guy is legitimately psychopathic, that the attack could very well have been genuinely random, that this was an attempted murder that he just wasn't quite quick enough to pull off. Based on this, I was thinking the guy was a drifter, and those guys tend to move on pretty quick. Apparently not this guy. So who did he do this time?"

The two glanced at Amanda again, who this time sensed it and matched both of their stares. Scott shrugged and said, "Lt. Quinn."

Colin tried to hide his surprise. He wasn't sure how successful he was. He had the feeling that it was as much a revelation for Amanda as it was for him.

"Why do you think they're connected?" Colin asked. Scott just stared back. Colin tried again. "Fine. But why would someone off a frat boy and a police lieutenant?" he asked, incredulous.

"That was where you were supposed to come in," Amanda said, her voice dripping with contempt. She looked at Scott and Sunny. "Sorry for the wasted trip, guys. I should have known better." Sunny shrugged. They turned to go into the garden shed and collect their things. Scott held up his hand. "I'm going to have a cigarette out here before we get back in the car." They closed the door to the shed, and Scott lit up.

Colin looked at the cigarette and licked his lips. He usually didn't allow himself to smoke, but his ego had been bruised. Amanda was the only woman he had ever known who could actually make him smart with a tongue-lashing. It was part of the reason he had ended the relationship. It was no good being with someone who could have that much of an effect on you. He managed not to ask for one, but he lingered for a moment to enjoy the smell.

Scott watched the door close behind the others and then drew in close to Colin "You want to catch this guy?" he asked as he exhaled, the words seeming to ride the puff of smoke. Colin was surprised but managed to bite back the desire to say something smart, and simply nodded. Scott eyed him a second more. "Give me your number." Colin gave it; Scott didn't bother to write it down or put it in his cellphone. "Cancel any plans you have for tonight."

"You know where he is?" Colin asked.

"No," Scott replied, "But I have a fair idea where he is going to be." He took another drag on his cigarette. "You got a gun?" he asked.

"Yeah."

Scott hesitated. "Do you have two guns?" Colin nodded.

"Bring your guns," Scott said.

~ ~ ~

This whole fucking thing had been a mess. Pike had not survived forty years as a businessman by making messes. What he had found as a man who kept one foot firmly on each side of the law, was that what both sides valued above everything else was subtlety. Plausible deniability. Everything worked just far enough out of sight, with just enough finesse, that at the end of the day, when they looked at themselves in their bathroom mirrors as they prepared to go to sleep, they didn't have to flinch at what stared back at them.

Of course, it was all bullshit. The kid who talked about fair trade and social justice blogged about it on an iPad made in China, wearing shoes that had been made someplace worse. The woman who talked about Christian values stiffed charities and slept with her husband's golf buddies. So long as the stink wasn't coming from their backyard, where all the neighbors could smell it, most people just plain didn't give much of a fuck what happened behind the scenes. Pike had been an operator and had survived three generations of heavy players, and the one core thing that never changed was that people didn't mind being rotten, they minded *knowing* that they were rotten. And they really minded *other* people knowing they were rotten.

As for himself, it was an aspect of his personality that Pike himself had come to peace with early in his life. It gave him the edge. He did what was necessary to achieve what he wanted, there was nothing more complicated to it than that. And for the most part, he achieved it.

But this mess had reminded some people that they were rotten. It had even come perilously close to reminding people that *he* was rotten. And that was something he could not tolerate. Even before the whole thing had started it had been a mess. He had been forced to send his own son, the stupid little shit, out of the country, not out of fatherly love, but out of self-love. If it ever came to light what that little cum-stain had done, he would be ruined. How was he supposed to predict that the aftermath of that event would be the real bitch?

The public suicide would have been bad enough, and certainly would have sent morale in Pike's own ranks plummeting for a while. He could deal with that, though. What he couldn't deal with was the mess the man Pike had chosen to clean up the *first* mess had caused. The man had been recommended by an old associate of Bingham's as being very dependable. By all accounts he kept a cool head; why had he chosen to wait until he worked with Pike to shit the bed? And then Quinn – to have one of his own lieutenants turn against him at such a time. To be forced to deal with it in this way. Truly, these were the times that tried men's souls.

Pike had men in the department trying to spin it as a simple home-invasion attempted robbery. He had even suppressed some troubling evidence of there being a third party in the house at some time during the incident. He couldn't deal with that now. Pike closed his eyes in frustration. If whoever saw what happened was dumb enough to stick their head up, Pike would be obliged to knock them down. Until then he would have to hope that whoever witnessed the event and somehow got away was smart enough to be scared shitless upon seeing a cop iced. If he hadn't come forward by now, he probably wouldn't.

Still, there was the proverbial light at the end of the tunnel. Quinn was dead, the evidence was destroyed, and now his men would meet the killer here in this little grove on one of Pike's ranches. There would be one more body on the foundations, the last loose end cut off and everybody could go home. Everybody but the loose end, that is.

The meeting was in a little hollow on one of Pike's ranches. It was a good place, a little bowl surrounded on all sides by hills, only one small dirt road, little more than a trail, leading into it. A pretty little copse of oak grew at its center. Pike sat there now with half a dozen men. Bingham leaned against the hood of the pickup truck Pike sat in; Flannigan sat in the passenger seat next to him, the late afternoon light gleaming off his bald head. Outside were a couple of Bingham's boys, eager to prove themselves, who had been brought in just in case. They were nervous, but trying to keep cool; two watched as a third did donuts on an ATV, limiting their comments to the occasional stream of tobacco juice. The sound of the whirring engine was annoying Pike, but he decided to let the kids keep at it. Gave them something to do, kept their minds occupied on something other than how scared shitless they were. It would be worth it.

Pike craned his neck forward looking down the dirt road; the man who called himself Spence wasn't late, not yet. He still had three minutes. The thing was, Pike had chosen this particular spot for their meeting for the excellent view it afforded – because of its high ground, and the single dirt road, you could see anybody coming from miles off. Spence wasn't coming. He should at least be in sight by now.

He looked down at his watch: two minutes to three. He gave a long sigh, tinged with disappointment. The rat fleeing wasn't the worst thing that could happen. He had done what he had been asked to do beforehand, at least. Still, Pike didn't like loose ends. He'd much prefer to watch the pigs remove his corporeal body from this Earth and take him completely out of the equation, than spend his time wondering if he'd pop back up someday. But he supposed there was nothing to be done for it. A canceled variable was a canceled variable after all. Even if it left him with a remainder.

He had just cleared his throat to tell Flannigan to start driving when the phone rang.

It wasn't his phone, which played the opening bars to "Mama Tried," and it wasn't Flannigan's, which played an insipidly thuggish cut of hip-hop. This was a harsh electronic squawk, the default ringtone of some cheap piece of plastic. Set on its full volume and vibration, it sounded as though some invisible bird was trapped inside the car, beating itself against the windows trying to get out.

Flannigan craned his neck around, searching the floor of the backseat. Pike felt the cuff of his left leg vibrate. He bent down and fished under the seat. His hand touched something slick. He tried to grab whatever it was, but it was stuck to the bottom of the seat. He understood – it was a nest of duct tape. His fingers found the edge and he pulled. The phone came free and dropped to the floor. Pike grabbed it.

It was small, black and nondescript, a little prepaid job that could be purchased at any convenience store in the world. Sure enough, it shuddered in his hand like a small animal trying to escape. The small message window read "Unknown caller." He pressed the green button to answer. A familiar voice was on the other end.

"I hope you don't mind me not coming out in person. I have an aversion to turkey shoots." The hit man's voice was high and reedy, slightly nasal and seemed to have a hook at the edge of every sentence it spoke. The voice of a cat or a fox in an old cartoon. The voice of someone who was very pleased with themselves.

"So long as you understand you're forfeiting the money by doing so," Pike answered, as calmly as he could.

"Oh, I wouldn't say that. In fact, I've raised my price." He said a number that had seven zeroes in it. Pike gave a horselaugh.

"Son, where do you come off?"

"Cut the shit, Pike I watched the video." That stopped him cold.

"I specifically told you-" Pike began.

"Yeah, and I specifically told you I was leaving town. That wasn't good enough for you, so here we are. Now don't try and tell me you don't have it. I know what you're worth and I know that guys like you always keep a lot of liquid cash on hand as a rainy-day fund. Well, partner, the clouds are converging. If you don't deliver the amount I specified where and when I tell you to, I'll start by sending copies to the local news. Sure, you might own them, but I'll send it to Santa Barbara and San Francisco too, for good measure. After that, I'll just go ahead and post it on YouTube, Vimeo, a few other places. I know you haven't seen it, Pike, so you'll have to take it from me: It's baaaad, Pike, I mean real bad, the worst picture you have in your head of it doesn't even begin to touch the reality. I think it has real potential, Pikey; you might go viral, as the kids say. It'll be as big as one of those cat videos everybody loves and if it gets out they're not even going to bother throwing you in prison. They'll lynch you from a fucking lamppost."

Pike could no longer contain his anger. "If you're so fucking good, then tell me who the fuck escaped you last night at Quinn's?"

There was a silence on the other end; Pike had finally scored a point. "I'll be dealing with them right after I deal with you, Pike, don't you worry about that. You just worry about the money. Which, by the by, I may burn. I just want you to lose something you actually care about."

Pike clenched his teeth. The knuckles on his hands had gone white, he could feel the phone straining beneath his fist; a few more pounds of pressure and it would shatter. "Where do you want it?" Pike finally managed to ask.

"I'll call and let you know." The voice said, "So don't lose that phone. There is one more thing Pike: Which of your men do you want me to kill?"

Pike's face went white. "What?" he whispered.

"Like I said, I've dealt with guys like you before. You're all the same, you demand shows of power. That was my mistake walking into the diner. Mea culpa, I won't make it again."

"You don't have to-" Pike began, but the voice cut him off.

"Look I know you think you're King of the Hayseeds, but I'm here to show you that you ain't even safe in the heart of your own Kingdom of Cowshit. Now, I was going to shoot the big'un from the diner, the one sitting next to you." Sweat broke out on Pike's forehead; he couldn't help but stare at Flannigan. Flannigan stared back, looking too confused to be scared. "Or maybe the ginger who hired me and wouldn't stop giving me the hairy eyeball. But I can't help but think you're attached to him, and I don't want you to take it too personal. Unless, of course, you're madder than I thought about him having hired me?"

"No," Pike said. "Not him."

"Well what about the little D-bag on the ATV who thinks he's on a playdate? He's probably scaring the cows and shit, I'd be doing you a favor." Pike was silent. "Pike." the voice had risen an octave, chastising now. "I want to hear that you're OK with this, otherwise I'm going to have to surprise you."

"Fine," Pike managed to choke out.

"Give me the all clear." Spence said. Pike could hear the smile in the fucker's voice.

"All ... clear."

A sudden crack broke the calm of the ranch. Bing dropped to his gut and crawled as far under the pickup as his body would allow. He didn't have to. The front of the kid's helmet spiderwebbed and he pitched over the handlebars of the four-wheeler. It ran him over with a sickening crunch that sounded to Pike almost as loud as the rifle. The two new kids let forth streams of vomit colored tobacco brown.

"Was that good for you too, Pike?" Spence asked, "I know it was your first time, so I tried to be gentle."

"If this doesn't go your way I'm going to beat you like a sick dog before you die," Pike hissed into the phone. But the line had gone dead. Pike threw the phone, and it bounced off the windshield to land in the back.

He got out of the car and walked around to where Bing's legs were sticking out from under the front of the truck. "Get up, Bing," Pike said. "You're making a goddamn fool out of yourself."

"What the hell is happening?"

"Nothing," Pike said contemptuously. "It happened. Get up." Bingham did, breathing hard, red all the way to his scalp, the front of his white T-shirt stained the red brown of the soil. He looked around as though he could see the sniper. "Stop that," Pike snapped.

"What the hell just happened?" Bingham asked.

"Never mind that," Pike said, "I need you to take every prospect you got and bring them in this afternoon. Get them off the farm team and into uniform. We are officially in war mode."

"What about him?" Bingham asked, pointing to the mangled body of the ATV rider.

"He have a family?" Pike asked.

"Just a momma, but she's in Chowchilla, and they don't talk much."

Pike considered this for a moment, and then nodded at the other two kids, who were looking pale and shaky, having yet to even wipe the sick off the front of their shirts. "Them two wanted to prove themselves. Have them feed him to the pigs."

~ ~ ~

It had been a hell of a day. Karl had woken up with the kind of hangover that his body occasionally sent him in order to angrily remind him that he was no longer nineteen. As though there was any danger of him forgetting.

He would have preferred to spend the day making his apartment as dark as he could, smoking a little pot to take the worst of the headache off and seeing what was on TCM. Unfortunately, before he could commence, his father called. The kid he'd hired had flaked out on him. He needed Karl's help.

So Karl walked out into the day, his glasses a pitiful shield against the light. Everything he did and saw made him want to flinch. He got into his dirty old GMC and fought with it for five solid minutes trying to get it to turn over. It finally did, and he was on his way. He stopped at a fast food drive-through because he didn't have time to get an actual breakfast. He had hoped that something in his stomach might help him out, but instead the grease just made him sick.

A few minutes later he was at the front gate of the country club. After being delayed another five minutes as the gatekeeper checked Karl out with a diligence that probably wasn't present at most border crossings, they finally let him through, though pretty soon Karl began to wish they hadn't.

His father was waiting for him, standing in front of the two-toned Chevy that he'd had since the '80s. The bed of the truck was filled with cedar chips, the smell of which made Karl's head ache. "Thanks for coming out, son. I'll make it up to you later this week," his dad said.

Karl managed to shake his head, said it wasn't necessary. Then he was up in the bed of the pickup shoveling the chips into a wheelbarrow that had been set below him. The cedar irritated his eyes and nostrils – the smell of it had always bothered Karl, but in his present condition it downright burned. After a few moments he had a full wheelbarrow. His forearms strained as he lifted it and took it around back to where his father was waiting. Karl dumped the barrow in front of his father, who began to spread the chips, then he went back to fill it again.

By the third barrowful Karl's sweat was falling freely, mixing with the cedar. He wiped his forehead with a handkerchief but the sweat still fell into his sensitized eyes, which stung, making him feel stupid and panicky like a deer trapped in a forest fire. His eyes began to water so badly he could barely see. Soon he was following the path to his father by memory as much as anything else.

After an hour the truck was empty. Karl's father went to fill it. Karl sat on the sidewalk, his shoulders sagging, and lit a cigarette. He had hardly gotten a drag of it when a woman in a tracksuit walking by on the other side of the street stopped and sniffed loudly. "Excuse me, sir?" she called out loudly, to make up the distance, the spin she put on the word sir like the twist of the knife. "Sir, would you put out your cigarette? This is a neighborhood with children in it."

Karl looked to his right and to his left. There was no one save himself and the woman present, let alone any children. "I believe it's a school day," he said.

The woman gave him a smile that made something inside Karl curdle, "Sir, I've asked you nicely. This is my home," she said, gesturing grandly across the street with the air of a feudal lord. "Not yours. Please put out your cigarette."

Oh it's your home all right, Karl thought, and what did you do for it? How long have you lived here? San Rita was Karl's home. He was willing to bet he had been there far longer than this woman who had the smell of carpetbagger and soft living wafting off of her. He briefly considered putting the cigarette out on her forearm, before he sighed and stubbed it out on the ground – not for her sake, but for his father's. Karl's truck bore the Winslow's Landscaping logo on it as well. And he could practically hear the gently admonishing "Karl ..." that his father gave him whenever he was worried he might piss off the other half.

"Thank you," she said sweetly, and continued huffing on her way, probably in a big hurry so she could go brag to her friends how righteously she'd put the hired help in its place. He darkly wished a cardiac arrest in her future.

His father returned with another load of cedar and they repeated the morning's labor, only this time it was hotter. His father drove off once more, returning this time with a truck full of manure and a bag of Taco Bell, the smells coming from both disturbingly indistinguishable.

"This should do us," the elder Winslow said, making it perhaps the twentieth word he had spoken through the day. Karl nodded his assent. They chewed thoughtfully through a few burritos and gorditas. Then Karl stripped down to his undershirt and climbed up into the truck again. The manure was loose and gave under his weight, so Karl couldn't find a place to stand that didn't leave him standing shin-deep in cow shit. He began to shovel.

The wind picked up and blew some of what he was shoveling back at him. The manure mixed with the sweat on his arms, chest and neck and began to burn. By the time he had delivered his fourth barrowful, his skin had turned an angry red where it wasn't covered by the dark brown dust. The wind picked up some more and blew some into his mouth. Karl gagged and spat in protest, but he couldn't get it all out. He tied his bandanna around his mouth and nose and redoubled his efforts, trying to work the grit from his mouth as he strained against the pile. He couldn't help but wonder how his life had ended up with him literally eating shit for a living. He couldn't get it out; the taste was still there. His arms were sore and the veins on them bulged, making the irritated red skin hurt more.

A car drove by – the fabled children back from school. It actually slowed as it passed, and Karl could almost hear the parent in the front telling his kids that if they didn't do well in school they'd end up like that. At the moment Karl couldn't rightly blame them. Though kids like that would never end up like him. Even if they were complete fuck-ups they would always have mommy and daddy's money to fall back on; they could live in their parents' basement and play video games until they were twenty-eight and no one would say boo about it. They'd never be forced to do anything as menial as physical labor.

He only had a few more loads to go when the SUV pulled into the driveway. There was a yellow ribbon on the back. A magnet – wouldn't want to leave any sticky residue on the paint. The woman driving it got out, carrying two shopping bags, and smiled at him. Karl lifted his hand and continued shoveling. The woman went in the front door.

Karl brought the load around and found the woman talking to his father, shaking her head at the work they had spent the day doing. A dog of indeterminate breed sat in the middle of the yard, panting happily. The woman started walking, Karl couldn't hear what was being said, but she pointed to places, shaking her head unhappily. Karl's father meekly followed a few steps behind her. Karl's father was a small man; Karl had gotten his height from his mother's side of the family. He said he was five and a half feet, but Karl doubted that he reached five-five now. He had begun to age in earnest, and a few more years would see him shrink even more. He hung his head now and looked for all the world like the world's oldest schoolboy on his way to write lines.

The dog turned and saw Karl, barked happily and then took a shit in the middle of the green lawn. The woman turned and pointed to it, and handed Karl's father a plastic bag. Karl watched as the old man made his way over to the pile of shit, and then bent down and picked it up with the plastic bag. The woman's lips were full and painted, and they smiled while he did it.

Karl felt a hatred for the woman so sudden and complete he didn't quite know how to take it. He saw in her the corrupt face of everyone who had ever kept him down. Everyone who had ever hired him to do work too dirty and unpleasant for their own hands. Everyone who cut funding to public schools while sending their own kids to private. The ones who sent him to that fucking desert while their sons went off to college.

But that wasn't the worst of it. The worst of it was that a deeper darker part of him found a flare of hatred for his own father as well, and all those like him who meekly acquiesced to his betters and picked up their shit with a thank you on their lips. All those like him who let this happen. He wished he could take that fucking magnet off the back of her gas-guzzler and make her eat it.

Instead he walked back and filled up another load. As he did he thought of his friend Randy, now dead six months. Randy, who had always blasted Steve Earle out of the Humvee and could recite any given stretch of Forrest Gump in its entirety; Randy, who had managed to survive two tours of active duty in the desert, but had not been able to survive two weeks working for these fucking people. He had gone to work for them at the country club in the Ohio rust belt former factory town where he had lived.

He had shot himself in his garage, wearing his dishwasher whites, the idea of going in for another day apparently too much for him to bear. His suicide note read simply "This is Endsville where all rail services terminate." It was a reference to a book Karl had not read. Karl had not been able to afford the trip out for his funeral. But he had sent flowers and spent the day it was held getting darkly drunk and thinking about memories he usually didn't allow himself to dwell on. There were so many others – Mike Jackson, shot down while on patrol in a marketplace; his best friend Harry Powell, blown up by an IED, half of his face melted like a candle, shipped out to Germany and then never heard from again.

The worst part about Randy was that it wasn't only sorrow and anger that he had felt when he heard of his friends' death. Down below those things was an ugly, insidious layer of satisfaction that made him hate himself but was no less present for it. Knowing that he was stronger, knowing that he wasn't going to be one of those burned-out vets who flamed out, because hell, if he was, it would have happened by now. He was no longer so sure.

After all, Randy's father had died just a little under a year before. Randy had loved his old man and wouldn't have done what he did if he had been around to hurt. Sure, Karl wasn't going to burn out today. But after his old man was gone? When the days like today began to stack up and bend him with their weight? Might he not one day sit in his garage like Randy did and decide that the whole charade of "normal" life was just too much of a fucking bother?

Thinking of his father, Karl was overcome by a crippling wave of shame. How dare he look down on his father, just because he was a man who understood that sometimes you had to bow to get on in this world? His father had created his own business. He'd carved out a place for himself and his family in a world that was harsh and bore no one mercy. So he bowed meekly and took a little shit – maybe you couldn't afford to be a firebrand when you had a family to suffer for your actions along with you.

Karl hadn't created anything for himself. What had he done but ride on his father's coattails? Just as much as those kids he had been mentally cursing out early. He had taken shelter in this safe place his father had carved out with his will. What did he know about it? He still did not understand the weight of years. He was still dependent on him for work and he had the gall to disdain him. What had he done for himself?

Karl's phone began to ring. He took it out and considered the number on the screen for a moment that felt a lot longer than it was.

Then he answered it.

~ ~ ~

The car ride back to the paper was mostly silent and very uncomfortable. It wasn't until they parked that Amanda spoke. "So are you guys going to tell me why you know details about the murder of a policeman?"

"I'd prefer not to," Scott said mildly.

"Would you like to tell me why you apparently aren't sharing this information with the police?"

"I'd prefer not to," Scott said.

Amanda wheeled on him. "And what would you say if I just called the cops myself, or Russell?"

"You won't do that," Scott said.

"And why not?"

"Because you're not an informer and you don't let other people solve your problems for you." Amanda stared back; Scott couldn't help but smile a little bit.

"Look, kid, I know it stings. You're smart. You might not know everything, but you do know that two people who have been in close proximity to Sunny and myself have both wound up dead, one a very important, capable man. Could you possibly concede that perhaps in keeping some information from you I'm trying to act in your best interest?"

"Last I checked, you're not my father and that's not your concern."

Scott shrugged. "Be that as it may, I'm the one holding the information here, and-"

"Quinn was involved in covering up the identity of the man who killed himself the other night at the paper." Sunny said. "The guy who died had evidence that implicated Jonathan Pike in something and was trying to get us to notice it. Quinn found it before we did, and tried to blackmail Pike. Pike had him killed. The guy who did it got away with the evidence against Pike. Pike's probably had it put through the shredder by now."

Scott shot Sunny a shocked glare that he shrugged off. "We're at a dead end," Sunny replied. "Any input is better than none. She's a big girl, she helped us out. If she wants in it's her decision." Scott scowled in reply.

"But that doesn't make sense," Amanda said.

"What doesn't?" Scott snapped.

"If this guy just wanted to bust Pike, why didn't he mail the evidence in? Leave it on your desk?"

"He didn't know who he could trust," Scott said. "Pike has people on the police force. I'm sure he has folks in the newsroom too. He probably wanted to expose it to as many people at once as possible. Make sure it couldn't just fall into the wrong hands and disappear. His mistake was that the wrong hands got to him first."

"You have to admit," Sunny said. "It made one hell of an impression."

"But it made the wrong impression," Amanda said. "Instead of making you look at Pike, it made you look at *him*. If he turns on Pike and tries to take him down, why kill himself? Why not try to see it through?"

"Maybe he figured that turning on Pike made him a dead man walking already," Sunny offered.

"Maybe he just did something he couldn't live with," Scott said. There was an awkward moment of silence in the car. Scott shrugged. "Either way, it's a dead end now."

Sunny looked at him suspiciously. "You're the one who said it," Scott said. "The ball is in their court, we just have to wait to see what happens."

~ ~ ~

Directly after finishing his business with Pike, Spence returned to his hotel room. It was about three-thirty; if he was efficient he could finish his scouting before his quarry got off work. After the clusterfucks the last two assignments had turned out to be, his professional pride was demanding a hitch-free job.

The phone book held a surprising number of Wans in the San Rita area, but, as he had hoped, not all that many Sunnys. There were in fact none in the phone book, but there were three S. Wans. Spence called the first and got no answer. He called the second and a woman picked up, introducing herself as Sandra. He hung up without speaking. The third number was answered by an elderly voice in what Spence thought was Mandarin before switching to profoundly broken English when Spence said, "Hello."

He decided to go to the first address.

A quick online map check later and he was on his way across town to an area near the college, filled with single-story, slightly dilapidated houses, cheap apartment buildings and slightly upscale condos. Student housing at its finest. He wondered why Wan hadn't moved on.

It turned out the address was for one of the condos. Spence parked a few blocks away, put on his false glasses and a dark beanie, and made his way to the complex. He ducked around the back to the complex's parking lot, making sure Wan's space was empty and walked around to the front. It was a nice place with a big, open, deeply shaded courtyard filled with palms and glass tables. Only a small pool, ugly and dirty, its surface covered in dead bugs and leaves, marred a feeling that was close to elegance.

The gate to the courtyard had a lockbox with a panel of numbers on it, but it had been propped open with a cinder block by some thoughtful individual, Spence stepped right in.

He made his way over to Wan's condo. He tried the door; it was locked. He quickly scanned the courtyard. Though he could hear the sounds of a loud TV, the yard itself was deserted and Spence could detect no eyes looking at him through blinded windows. He reached into his coat pocket and pulled out a ring of skeleton keys. He found Wan's model on the third try.

He entered the foyer. The condo was smaller than it looked from the outside. The first floor contained only a living room and a kitchen, both neat but cozy, filled with the little things that accrue when a place has been lived in long enough to call home. Two sizable bookshelves filled with contemporary lit like Frazen and Chabon, a shelf full of comics with titles like "Sandman" and "Scott Pilgrim," and two thick shelves of crime novels and Stephen King that Spence guessed belonged to Wan. The books all looked pretty well-thumbed, aside from a row of thick classics that lay on the bottom shelf like a foundation and had a distinct layer of dust on them.

An Xbox and a stack of video games lay next to a fairly expensive looking TV, next to which was another bookshelf, this one filled with DVDs. There were a fair amount of chick flicks on the DVD shelf and, like the bookshelves, there was a distinct his-and-hers vibe. Spence hoped Wan had a woman; it would be easier to find out the name of the second man that way. Men with women were always easier to break than men without women. He had held fire to the bottoms of men's feet before and had them keep their silence, only to have their resolve break like china cups when the possibility of harm coming to their girlfriend was mentioned.

The kitchen was similarly neat, a spice rack and butcher's block, the cupboards and refrigerator filled with organic and fair trade food. Pictures on the fridge confirmed the presence of the woman, an artsy-looking girl whose hair was an alarming shade of red and who had her arm slung around Sunny in most of the pictures, save for a few of their respective families. Spence made his way upstairs. The carpet covering them was thick and Spence noted with satisfaction that they did not creak under his weight.

The upstairs consisted of a small bathroom whose scented soaps, candles and lotions removed any doubts about the feminine presence in the house. Next to it was a bedroom that had been turned into a small studio, which belonged to the girl. Spence took his time there, examining the stack of CDs next to a small portable player, everything from Ani DiFranco to Arcade Fire, and examining the canvases, which ranged from slightly impressionistic landscapes to full-on abstractions. He spent perhaps five minutes considering the unfinished canvas that was propped on an easel in the middle of the room. It was a figure, unmistakably female but distended and malformed, against a black background. He looked closer at the tentative pencil sketches that spread from the figure, etching patterns against the dark. He wondered if she would have time to finish it before he killed her. He hoped so; she was not without talent.

Lastly, he walked across the hall to the master bedroom. Dominated by a bed and two chests of drawers on opposite sides of the room, it did not feel as personal as the other rooms. He walked to one wall and rapped against it, and then to the other. Both came back gratifyingly solid. The shots from his silenced pistol would not be heard by the neighbors. The interrogations might be slightly more problematic. He would have to make sure that when he woke Sunny up he saw the gun immediately, and he would have to impress upon Sunny the importance of his girlfriend's cooperation. If she woke up and screamed he would have to kill them both right away, and then he would be without a lead on the old man.

He stood by the bottom-right corner of the bed and drew his thumb and forefinger into an imaginary pistol. From this vantage point he covered the bed in its entirety. He took a deep breath, envisioned the act and then walked out of the house, careful to lock the door behind him.

He didn't leave right away. Instead, he waited in his car, near the entrance to the parking lot, and waited for half an hour until a small silver Honda pulled into Wan's space. The woman got out – there was a slight sag to her shoulders; it had been a long day at whatever job she worked. There would probably be no work done on the canvas tonight. A pity. She stopped and looked around, like a deer in a glade who catches the smell of people. Spence sat still in his car. He wasn't worried. He had witnessed this phenomenon in his quarry before; he was confident of his blind.

Sure enough, the moment passed and the girl continued towards her house. See you tonight, Spence thought and started the car as soon as she was out of sight.

~ ~ ~

The night came on quickly. Sunny cooked a chicken stir-fry heavy on the bell peppers. The two of them ate quietly in front of an episode of *"Parks And Recreaction";* they were both tired. After returning from Avalon, Sunny had set to finishing his work. But he felt distracted and irritated, and the articles he was working on took him much longer than usual. He hated to admit it, but he had gotten caught up in this thing, and to see the trail suddenly die so quickly, when he felt in the very midst of things, bothered him.

The events of the last few days had been so completely counter to the normal rhythms of his life that to have them vanish so suddenly was in its own way just as disturbing as their occurrence. It was as if a monster had reared its head into Sunny's field of vision, and then disappeared as soon as he blinked. Seeing as it had neither pounced on and devoured him nor been dispatched with fire and a stake through the heart, Sunny was left with just the unresolved anomaly. It was all the more unsettling for being out of sight. It had settled into his brain like a permanent itch on his peripheral vision.

He didn't see Scott again that day. When Sunny went by his desk after finishing his work, he was gone, leaving only the stale scent of cigarette smoke behind him. Sunny looked down at his desk for a moment in contemplation. He didn't know what he made of Scott. Had you asked him a few days before, he would have shrugged. Just another co-worker who he got along with alright. Some of others in the office made fun of his drinking, but Sunny had never seen any evidence of it interfering with the job. His copy was unspectacular, but it got the job done and was never inaccurate. He was old school to the core. They just didn't have much to say to each other. He would clap when he collected his gold watch in five to fifteen years and then would never think about him again.

Sunny had come to realize that the Scott he had known for the last two days was somebody new. He had been lurking in this other Scott the entire time, dormant but present. The problem was that, though Sunny felt that he had the old Scott pretty well pegged, he did not know what to make of this new one. He was of a type that Sunny had met only a few times before and it had never ended well: A dependable person who you could not trust.

It was those last words he had spoken in the parking lot that troubled Sunny – the phrase about them making the next move. Hiding behind those innocuous words was a certainty that there would be a next move. The fact that he had not deigned to share with Sunny what that next move might be formed the core of his anxiety.

As he gathered his things and started to leave the office, Amanda caught his eye. He shook his head, with a slight shrug. No new developments. Like Sunny, she looked slightly downcast. He imagined she must be feeling the same thrill of disruption that he did, and the odd pang of withdrawal. He did not know exactly why he had brought her in on this, and Sunny was a micro-analyzer by nature. She was smart, and he felt a new perspective would be helpful. Even though it had not panned out, he felt confident that it had been the right thing to do.

Since he had arrived home, Alicia seemed oddly disturbed as well, but when he pressed her she could come up with no reason for it beyond an unusually long day at work. Sunny could not tell if he was spreading disquiet to her or she to him, because the rest of the night was filled with a disturbing stillness that any other night would have passed for normalcy. After dinner and washing he tried to ring Scott. Sunny wasn't sure if the number he had been given was a cell or home phone. Either way it rang until Scott's gruff voice came on the line, a terse answering machine message. Sunny didn't leave one.

~ ~ ~

Scott looked at the phone on the wall and wondered for the hundredth time if he was doing the right thing. It was a thought, that was all; even less than a thought: an instinct. If he told the kid and it turned out he was wrong, the kid would be looking over his shoulder for the rest of his life. He liked the kid; he didn't want to do that to him.

And if he was right? If he was letting the kid walk blindly into a situation that could get him and his nice girlfriend killed? His ex-wife always said he had a funny way of showing his affection.

He paced in his trailer. The trailer had never seemed small until now, he realized he had no place to go in it. His hands shook. He hadn't had a drink all day. There was a certain nervous energy Scott had that the drinking tamped down. Since he didn't have that option, he had to be careful not to do anything stupid. He couldn't go out too early and blow the whole thing. This was his last chance. Like it or not, there was something big here. Every instinct told him he was right on the cusp of a precipice, and if he could look down and truly see how high up he was the magnitude of his vertigo might send him sprawling. Whatever was on that disc had driven one man to kill himself and had turned a hardened homicide cop into a drunken, red-eyed mess. It had ruined everyone who had looked at it, and still Scott had to know.

That was what had driven Scott to be a reporter, that need to know. His mother had been a Bible thumper and had read to Scott many times the story of Sodom and Gomorrah to impress upon him what she called "the wages of wickedness." That hadn't been what had Scott had taken away from the story, though. It was the image of Lot's wife turned to salt when she looked back to see what Jehovah did when he could not find ten righteous men. Warned by her husband and the angels not to look, but not being able to help it. Scott knew that if he were walking beside them and felt the heat on his back, he too would be helpless to do anything but turn and behold. Damn the consequences. Or as his father used to tell him, usually right before he belted him one, "You'd stick your head in the fire if someone told you you could see hell that way."

Scott abruptly stopped. He wasn't one to dwell on the past, but the lack of drink was sending his mind to strange places. And if ever he had to focus, if ever he had to be in the here and now, it was tonight. He looked at the clock. Almost ten. He would call Colin make sure he was ready.

~ ~ ~

It was one in the morning when Spence crossed the threshold into Sunny's house. It was a quiet night, no keggers at any of the nearby houses. Spence breathed deeply, holding the scent of those he was after for a long moment. He stood in the foyer; the door closed behind him, and he listened. There was nothing – no TV, no radio, not even the ticking of a clock; they were all electric in the Wan household.

Spence reached under his coat and withdrew the silenced pistol. Also under his coat was a roll of duct tape, a butterfly knife and a gag, in case Wan really did make him cut on the woman. Table salt and alcohol he could find in their home. Spence didn't think he would need them, but he found it best to follow the Boy Scout motto: always be prepared.

Satisfied that his quarry was asleep and with his night vision well on the way to developing, Spence began to walk up the stairs, taking them slowly, a step at a time carefully laying his weight on each. The steps did not betray him.

He reached the top of the stairs and stood before the closed bedroom door. He closed his eyes one more time, took a deep breath and centered himself, like a diver on the highboard. His eyes snapped open. He held the pistol up. He was ready.

"I wouldn't," said a voice. Spence was not by nature a man who spooked easily, but he had to work to stifle a cry. The voice came from a shape at the end of the hall leading to the studio. His vision sharpened and the shape came into focus: A man in a chair with a Glock pointed casually at Spence. Not just any man, but the one from last night.

Spence stood stock-still, the adrenaline pumped through him with such ferocity that he felt he might burst.

If he played this right he would have all of his messy business taken care of in one night.

"I know what you're thinking," the man in the chair said, his voice even and calm, but with an undercurrent of excitement that Spence recognized. "Even if I've got the drop on you there's still a chance you can outdraw me. That's a possibility I will allow ..."

Spence suddenly felt a cold pressure on the back of his head, and at the very corner of his peripheral he could see a younger man behind him arm outstretched. He was unsure what kind of gun was pressed to his head.

"But not him," the man in the chair concluded.

"What now?" Spence asked.

"Why don't you start by putting the safety on your weapon and dropping it to the floor," the man in the chair suggested.

Spence did as he was told, then he whipped around with his butterfly knife, batting the younger man's forearm away, twisting around as he turned he gripped it and pinned it to the man's side with his left while he stabbed out with his right.

The man had made an amateur mistake and gotten too close, leaving himself with no leverage and nowhere to run. Spence's stab was wild, though – it glanced off his ribs and then drew down his side, unseaming him with a long gash but hitting nothing crucial. The young man screamed, shrill and panicked. The sound hit something in Spence; he had to finish him. The old man wouldn't shoot for fear of hitting his accomplice, he had to cross the hall to get at Spence – that gave Spence just a few more seconds to find the boy's neck and open it. The young man was struggling; his flailing arms struck Spence and knocked off his glasses. Spence didn't notice. He raised his knife.

Just then the door beside him opened and light flooded the hallway, temporarily blinding Spence. A startled Sunny, in boxer shorts and nothing else, looked at them all in bewildered astonishment.

"Hit him!" Spence heard the old man cry, and only then did he see the baseball bat in Sunny's hand. Sunny stared at the old man with scarcely less astonishment than he did at Spence and the young one.

"Fucking HIT HIM!" the old man called again. This time Sunny snapped to, and for the second time in twenty four-hours, Spence watched as a bat wielded by Sunny Wan swung towards his face.

~ ~ ~

The assassin was out cold, and before Sunny could ask a question Scott had crouched down and begun to search him. Scott hadn't actually hoped that the assassin would have the disc on him, but stranger things had happened.

All the color drained from Sunny's face when they opened his coat and found the tape and gag there. Then he took a swing at Scott, cracking him a good one on the jaw. Scott fell back on his ass and lay there sprawled over the unconscious killer looking up at Sunny, rubbing his jaw, but not retaliating.

"You fucking knew he was coming here?" Sunny spat out.

"I didn't know," Scott said, but he looked away. "I just had a suspicion. I didn't want to spook you if it was nothing."

"No, you wouldn't want to do that," Sunny said. "You'd just rather let me and my girlfriend stay in the sights of a psychopath and then break into my house."

"I didn't break in," Scott said. "I saw you use the hedgehog."

"I really don't give a fuck about that right now, Scott." Sunny said, his voice rising high as he said it. "That is literally the least of my concerns." He pointed to the crumpled mass on the floor. "How the fuck did he find me?"

"Your picture's in the paper every day." Scott said. "After he had your name, the rest would be child's play."

Sunny shook his head and hit the wall. Alicia had come out into the hallway. She had wrapped herself up in a bathrobe. Her hair was disheveled, her eyes wide and confused.

"May I suggest," Colin said through a gasp of pain. "That we have more pressing matters to attend to?"

That seemed to snap Alicia out of whatever shock she was in. "I'll call the police," she said.

"Wait, don't," Scott said. She stopped, confused.

"This isn't your house. This isn't your call," Sunny said.

Scott propped himself up on his elbows and then got to his feet, "If you call the cops, we lose our chance to find out what's really going on." He pointed to the shallowly breathing body on the floor. "Besides, we might get some of Pike's men, and for all we know they'll just come help him finish the job."

"What the hell are you talking about?" Alicia asked. She turned to Sunny – there was hurt in her eyes along with the confusion now. Neither of them answered her.

"Look, the second he wakes up he is going to be a danger to us again," Scott said. "Let's neutralize him now, and then we can talk." Sunny nodded. Scott jerked his head toward Colin. "He's in no condition to exert himself. Will you help me carry him downstairs?"

There was something in Scott's voice that was almost like pleading. Sunny nodded. They took Spence downstairs, bound his wrists and ankles together and tied him tightly to a chair. Then they went back upstairs.

Colin was standing in the bathtub with his shirt off. The gash was about eight inches long down the ribs. It was long and ugly, but it seemed shallow. It was bleeding freely.

Colin gave Sunny a grin that was almost sheepish. "I think I managed to keep my blood off your carpet." Sunny shook his head, still stunned. There were some sentences one just didn't expect to hear. Alicia hurried into the room and handed him an old towel. Colin took it gratefully and pressed it to his side. It quickly turned red.

"Should we take you to the ER?" she asked.

Colin shook her head, "It's not as bad as it looks. If I could trouble you for some rubbing alcohol and gauze I should be able to take care of it right here."

Sunny followed her out into the hall. He put his hand on her shoulder. "Are you alright?" he asked.

She turned on him. It wasn't anger that he saw in her eyes, just a deep hurt, and suddenly he felt sick and ashamed.

"How did this happen?" she asked.

"It's a long story," Sunny said lamely.

"I assumed that much," she said. It was good to see a bit of her sarcasm back, a bit of *her* back; he had to suppress a smile. It was the first thing that made him feel good that night. "I mean how did it get this far without you telling me about it?"

Sunny looked away. "It all went so crazy so fast. I couldn't find a good time to say anything, and today I thought it was over, and just decided to leave it. By the time I found out it wasn't, I was standing in the hallway with a bat." He closed his eyes. "I just don't know how it got this far."

She drew his face to hers and looked him in the eye. "A man came into my home to hurt me. This is not OK."

"I know," Sunny said, and suddenly the weariness and the shame went away, replaced by a great burning anger. He wanted to go to the bound man downstairs and stomp the life out of him. He wanted to slit his throat and put his body somewhere where it would never be found. He wanted to grind him under his foot like the loathsome slug he was. How dare he? Alicia was still looking at him.

"I know you're in the middle of this," Alicia said. "And at this point the only way out is through. But we're going to need to figure this out when it's all over." Sunny nodded. Alicia leaned up and kissed him on the cheek and put her arms around him.

"I'm so thankful you're safe," was all Sunny could say. He held her for a moment longer. Then he heard the sound of a throat clearing. Both he and Alicia turned to see Scott standing there.

"I'm sorry to interrupt," he said. "But I wanted to let you know I'm going to call Amanda."

Sunny was stunned. "What, why?"

"She's in it now, no good for her to be walking around half-blind."

"Yeah, withholding important information from someone involved in this would really be a shitty thing to do," Sunny said. Scott had the decency to turn red. Sunny threw up his hands. "Fine, bring her in, might as well. We need every good mind we've got to get us out of this clusterfuck."

~ ~ ~

Scott sat across from the hit man in the twin of the chair to which he was bound. The floor in Sunny and Alicia's kitchen was a light blond hardwood. It looked expensive, not like the cheap linoleum in Scott's trailer. He hoped, if things got rough, they wouldn't scratch up the floor too badly.

115

Scott sat hunched over on the edge of the seat, hands together like a man in prayer – though men in prayer aren't usually gripping a Glock. His sleeves were rolled up to expose surprisingly bulky forearms. His hair was swept back, held in place by the glasses perched on his forehead. He looked like a stockbroker who had just negotiated a tough deal.

Of, course the negotiating had yet to commence. Colin and Sunny were both out of sight, listening from the living room. They had all decided to give Scott first crack at the man alone, figuring that a single man would be less predictable and give the man in the chair less to play with.

Colin was looking a little pale, now dressed in a Sun Records T-shirt of Sunny's a size too big. He had forced down a quart of Orange Juice to help steady himself after the blood loss. He had a kind of grim determination etched on his face. Amanda had arrived a few minutes ago and seemed nearly as incensed at having been kept out of the loop as Sunny and Alicia had been. One thing was for sure – tonight had won Scott no new friends. But he was used to that. There was no time to think about that now anyway, no good thinking about repercussions. Only time for the task at hand.

The hit man gave a low moan, the second he had given in as many minutes. Scott had to be careful not to assume anything. For all he knew the man had been conscious the entire time.

The man raised his head. He blinked at Scott, his eyes bleary. He looked around the room slowly; it took a moment for him to get back to Scott, and when he did his eyes finally focused. His upper lip rose unconsciously, baring his teeth like a dog's, and for a moment Scott saw his true face and was frightened. More frightened then he had ever been while the man was actually shooting at him.

Jesus, Scott thought, if I had sense I would just put a bullet in his face right now.

Scott had been in the presence of evil men before. This was different. Evil was a presence. This man was an absence, or perhaps more accurately an abscess – a stinking, festering piece of humanity that had spoiled. He was a void, a sucking hole of a man that Mark Quinn and that boy downtown and God knew how many others had disappeared into.

They regarded each other in silence for a moment. It was the bound man who broke it.

"Well?"

Scott decided to be direct. "What was on the disc you destroyed?"

"What disc?" the man asked, an exaggerated look of confusion on his face.

"The disc you destroyed for John Pike. The one Mark Quinn and Harper Lewis died over."

"Oh, that disc," the man said, his eyes widening in mock enlightenment. "See, I was confused, because I haven't destroyed that disc at all. It's totally intact, safe as houses."

"I don't believe you," Scott said.

"That's alright with me."

"You're Pike's man, he hired you to destroy whatever was on that disc. Why wouldn't you?"

"I was never Pike's man, I'm an independent contractor."

"Contractors don't get work by blowing up the kitchen they were designed to remodel."

"True, but they don't get good work by allowing themselves to be fucked over, either. Pike violated the terms of our contract, and when I canceled it he thought he'd play me. I've stuck around to teach him the error of his ways."

"Then why come after us?"

He seemed genuinely confused by the question. "Personal security, of course. Just because I'm no longer working for Pike doesn't mean witnesses suddenly stop being a threat to me. You and your friend were just at the wrong place at the wrong time."

"What about the boy downtown, how did he fit into all this?"

The man in the chair tried to shrug, but found he couldn't with his arms pinned to his sides, "That? Recreation." Scott knew that was the truth. He suppressed a shudder.

"What was on that tape, anyway?" Scott asked.

The man in the chair gave a hideous smile, "Well, I could tell you, but to get the full effect I think you really have to see it for yourself."

~ ~ ~

"Let me put this into perspective for you." Amanda said, "You are talking about going to the lair of a serial murderer. In the company of said serial murderer. Without telling the police or anyone else."

"That's about the sum of it," Colin agreed.

Amanda ignored him and stared directly at Sunny and Scott, "You don't think he has some kind of contingency? You don't think he's planned for this? You guys got lucky tonight. If you give him the home turf, let him work you on his ground, how much do you want to bet you won't get lucky again? You're not gunmen, you're writers, for Christ's sake. He's a mass murderer."

"I'm a gunman," Colin said.

"You're an idiot." Amanda replied without looking at him.

"You're right," Scott said. He sat slumped on the couch, his thumb and forefinger rubbing the bridge of his nose. He looked up and met Amanda's eyes. "But what else are we supposed to do?"

"Call the police," Amanda said.

"Yeah," he scoffed, "and watch the evidence disappear a second time. You think Quinn was the only cop that Pike had on the payroll? You think he doesn't have them on red alert right now, looking for that very thing?"

"They can't all be dirty," Amanda said. "You've been the crime reporter for twenty years. You've got to have some cops you can trust some you could call."

"I do," Scott allowed. "But until yesterday Mark Quinn would have been at the top of that list." He held up his hands. "All I know is that if we stop here, call the cops and have them arrest that thing in the kitchen, the trail ends. Pike gets away and we never even find out what crime he's gotten away with." He sighed, and then looked up and met the eyes of everyone in the room. "And I don't know about you all, but that goes against every single instinct I have. I'm no one to give a sermon, but I started as a journalist because I believed it was the one place where the search for truth was still possible."

Sunny stood up, and looked at Alicia for a long moment. "So we go," he said.

Scott looked up at him, and for a moment Sunny was sure he saw gratitude on the old guy's face.

~ ~ ~

Scott drove. Spence sat next to him looking forward; his eyes showed no distress, nor any real interest. There was a reptilian stillness to him that Scott could not help but find unnerving. They had buttoned him into a pea coat to hide the duct tape. His legs were free but his wrists were still bound together, his arms pinioned to his sides. Amanda, Sunny and Colin had all crammed into the backseat. Three kids on the way to the beach. Colin sat behind Spence, his gun at the ready, but Spence made no movements.

They had not brought Alicia. By tacit agreement they understood that, one way or the other, all four of them had signed on for this. They had bought their tickets and the time for a refund had long passed. Whatever happened to them happened. Alicia had not asked for this, though, and if something should happen to her or someone take a hold of her, all bets would be off.

The car was quiet, except for Spence's occasional statements of "left" or "right." He hadn't told them where they were going, only that it was not isolated. After about ten minutes of driving they came to a rundown motel near the college on a street that was full of them. "Stop here," Spence said.

They parked in an empty spot. The "No Vacancy" sign was on and the office was dark. No one saw them cross the parking lot. As they climbed the stairs they heard no noise, not even the sound of a too-loud TV or illicit hookup. It was dead. They stopped in front of room 217, Spence in the center, the rest flanking him.

"The key card is in my front pocket," Spence said, with a nod of his head to indicate which one.

Sunny leaned over and reached his hand into Spence's front pocket, trying not to imagine that he was reaching into the mouth of a hungry dog. But instead of teeth or a naked razor, Sunny only found the cool plastic of a key card. He slipped it into the electronic lock. It turned green.

~ ~ ~

Tony Ruiz didn't know why it was worth a c-note to Bing Earle for him to sit in the parking lot of this motel all night and take note of everyone who came in and out of it. Frankly, he didn't want to know. Earle's money spent, and he didn't have a better way to spend his time that night. He knew that much, and it was enough.

He spent the night listening to an Elmore Leonard novel on CD that he had picked up at the library, working on a book of Sudoku puzzles and washing down a big bag of Corn Nuts and a pack of jerky with a few tallboys. There were worse ways to pass an evening.

He hadn't expected much, and he had been rewarded. He had the sketch of the man he was looking for on his passenger seat, and though many pug-ugly white people had passed him by that night, this particular one had not. In fact, hardly anyone had passed by at all in the last few hours. He had worked through the first half of the book and now had to cheat to finish the puzzles more often than not.

From what he'd heard, Bing had paid a dozen other guys to do just what he was doing. He was just part of the net, that was all. Tony had contemplated skipping out early but decided against it. It wasn't likely that Bingham would come check on him, but it was possible. And once you were on Bingham Earle's shit list you tended to stay there, and it wasn't exactly a healthy place to be. Better bored and alive than entertained and dead.

Tony was just contemplating opening his third tallboy of the night when a car, a beat-up late-modeled Volvo, drove into the lot. The driver's side opened and an older man stepped out. He jerked his head around like a prairie dog and then rapped on the car roof. Three people piled out of the back. Only then did the passenger door open and the last person in the car emerge. The others surrounded him, like an entourage around a celebrity. It was tough to make out who he was from across the parking lot. Even harder with this crowd obscuring him from view.

But Tony's car lay directly between the group and the row of motel rooms. He turned off the volume on the audiobook and hunkered down in his seat. The people remained clustered around the mystery man as though they were guarding him. But for just a moment the man turned and looked at Tony's car as though he sensed him, and Tony saw him clearly. There was no doubt about it, this was the man Bing was after.

Tony managed to keep his cool. He stayed hunched down until he saw the five people enter their motel room and shut the door. Then he wrote down their room number on his hand, jogged to the nearest trash can, tossed his empties and called the number Bing had given him, careful to keep the slur out of his voice. Bing told him to sit tight and make sure no one left – he would be there presently.

~ ~ ~

Sunny wasn't sure what kind of chamber of horrors he had expected, but when they flicked on the weak light the room looked like any ordinary cheap motel room. Cracked plaster, cheap TV bolted to the cabinet, bad pictures on the walls and the smell of disinfectant wafting in from the bathroom. The man who called himself Spence seemed to sense this, as he disquietingly seemed to sense so many things, and turned to him. "Disappointed?" he asked with a smile.

Sunny could not help but feel a kind of revolted fascination with this little empty man who had nearly taken his life, and Alicia's. It was the same fascination that a man who has decided against suicide might find with the noose he has prepared, or the survivor of a head-on collision might hold for the two pieces of twisted metal he had just walked away from. This insignificant little object was almost the end of me? It seemed cosmically, comically stupid.

"Sit there," Colin said, shoving Spence into a cheap seat by the door. He drew his gun and pointed it at Spence. "Anything funny and I'll punch your fucking card," he said.

Spence reacted to this, as he had to all of Colin's tough-guy attempts, by not saying anything. He didn't even look at Colin, but looked past him off into the middle distance. Sunny wondered what he was seeing there and decided he would rather not know.

"Where's the disc?" Scott asked.

Spence inclined his head towards the bed. A laptop lay on it. "Right there. All nice and ready for you." Scott walked over to the bed and opened the laptop. It had been in sleep mode and a login screen greeted him. "The password is Bacon," Spence called. "Capital B." Scott typed it in. The desktop opened.

The screen that greeted them was blue and blank. There was no wallpaper background, not even the cheesy default featuring a plant or a sunset. The desktop itself was as uncluttered and blank as its master's face. Only a few Excel files titled "Expenses" and "Schedule" and a few default programs, nothing else.

Scott opened up the directory and found the disc. There was only one item on it, a movie file titled "Insurance." Scott highlighted it and was about to double-click when Spence spoke from behind him.

"You may want to give your lady friend a chance to leave the room," Spence said. "The content on that tape is quite disturbing, and considering it's me saying that ..."

Scott glanced over at Amanda, who shook her head. Then he turned back to the computer, took a deep breath and double-clicked. The video opened in full screen.

~ ~ ~

The footage was shaky at first; made on a cheap camcorder. The camera went up to the night sky, then came back down. It switched to night vision, casting everything in uncanny neon green, then switching back to normal view where it was too dark to make anything out, before ultimately settling to a low-light mode that made everything look washed-out, like a photograph left in the sun.

The camera settled down a bit, though it would still occasionally give a disconcerting jerk. It was a dark night but the area they were in was not without light. Big sodium arc lights that stood around the edge of a pit. At first Scott thought it might be a construction site, but then he recognized the terrain. It was the Coldwater Canyon Landfill fifteen miles out from San Rita. There was an annoyed grunt from off-screen.

"Bing," a young voice called out. "Come help me, this thing is heavy." Bing set the camera down, his boot briefly coming into frame. Then there was the sound of grunting and something came down in the foreground. Bing bent down and picked the camera back up. He began to focus it, and the frowning face of Harper Lewis came into view. "What are you doing with that?" Harper asked.

"Nothing," answered the voice of Bing. "Just making a little insurance."

"I don't think Mr. Pike would ..." Harper said slowly.

"Oh, I know Mr. Pike won't like it," Bing said. "But what you don't know is that Mr. Pike keeps a file of dirt on each and every one of us that works for him. Insurance, so we don't turn on him. I'm just getting a little insurance of my own. You need to get an umbrella before it rains. Now open the cooler."

"But Mr. Pike said-" Harper started.

"Boy, if I hear about Mr. Pike one more time I cannot be held responsible for my actions. Now open the fucking cooler." The camera tilted away from Harper towards the shape that had briefly obscured the camera before. It was a cooler, a big one. It had been wrapped in duct tape.

Harper came briefly into frame again. He opened up a box cutter and worked it around the lip of the cooler. When it finally came free, he hesitated a moment. "Go on, boy, open it!" Bingham said. Harper took a deep breath and pulled back the lid. Bingham hovered over him with the camera, like a vulture.

A girl looked up into the camera from inside the cooler. Harper gave a low moan of horror. The girl had been bound. Twine rope held her at the ankles, knees and wrists. Her wrists had bled a little where they had chafed. Her mouth had been sealed with a strip of duct tape. The girl had been crying. Dark streaks of mascara ran down her cheeks and snot had dripped down onto the gag. Bing's camera caught all the detail with unseemly appetite.

She began speaking before Harper had taken the gag all the way off. "Please," she said. "Please, I understand now that this was all a big misunderstanding. Just like the man said, and if you let me go I won't say anything because I understand that nothing really happened."

"ShhhShhhhShhh," Bing said, as if he were trying to calm a spooked animal. "I'm here to help you." She looked into the camera then up past it at Bing. Her eyes were frightened, mistrustful, but there was something there. That was the worst part of it, Scott would decide later. That was the part that would keep him up nights when it was all over, that would wake him from a sound sleep at three in the morning. She hadn't yet given up hope.

"Will you help me get out?" she asked, holding up her bleeding wrists.

"In a moment," Bingham said. "First I need you to tell me what happened."

"But–" she said.

"People may be coming," Bingham said. "I need you to tell me your story as quick as you can. What's your name?"

She looked into the camera. "It's Mia," she said, "Mia Hill."

"Mia?" Bingham said, his voice maddeningly smooth. "I need you to be brave for a minute and tell me what happened."

She swallowed and looked into the camera, "I came into town from Bakersfield for a party. My friend goes to college here. We went to this house party at the edge of town. A big house, it didn't look like it belonged to some college kid. I asked my friend how she knew this guy. He said they were in the same class." She took a deep, ragged breath to steady herself for what came next. "She introduced me to him. We started talking. He flirted with me, I thought he was cute. I started drinking, we danced a few time, and then he went to get us drinks and I-" she shuddered and stopped talking.

"He raped you?" Bingham prodded.

The girl nodded.

"And that man was John Pike Jr."

She nodded again.

"I need you to say yes," Bingham pressed.

"Yes," she said, her voice cracking. "It was John Pike Jr. He raped me."

"And what happened then?" Bingham asked.

"He, he ..." she took another deep, wet breath to center herself. "I woke up and he was gone. I went to my car."

"Did you see your friend?" Pike asked.

Mia shook her head. "No, she left me." Her voice cracked with sorrow.

"What did you do?"

"I drove to the police. A man came out and spoke to me."

"What was his name?"

"Matt," she started. "No Mark, It was Mark Quinn. He asked me to tell him what happened, and I did. At first he tried to play it off like it was a big misunderstanding, like he was on the guy's side. Asking me if I was sure it wasn't consensual, how much alcohol I had, if I was 21 or not. He asked me if I had any witnesses, but I wouldn't shake. So he started asking how I got here. Where I was from, whether my family knew I was here. I told them I snuck out for the party, and then ..."

She stopped, and a look of outrage filled her face. It was the outrage of a secure suburban girl who had been told all her life that the police were her friends and if she stayed a good girl they would always help her. It was the outrage of someone who had been betrayed. "Then he hit me, and I woke up here."

"Thank you, Mia," Bingham said. "You've been very brave." Then he turned to Harper. "Seal her back up."

The girl let out a shriek filled with such despair that it was all Scott could do not to cry out in sympathy. It tore at his heart. She cried, called for someone, anyone to help her, and lashed out with her arms. They struck the camera, which flew a few yards away. Landing at a skewed angle, the auto-focus shifted continuously during the next few seconds, but it was clear enough to make out what was happening. Bingham cocked back his arm and punched into the box full force. There was a sickening thud, the sound of a hammer hitting meat, and the girl inside stopped struggling. Bingham reached over and tucked her limp arms back into the box in a way that was almost gentle. Then he picked up the lid, and closed it with a firm push. He turned to Harper. "Come on, Harp, time to finish the job."

"Do we have to?" Harper pleaded. "Can't we just let her go? She said she wouldn't tell nobody."

"No." Bingham's voice made a hatchet chop out of the syllable.

"What about her friend? She didn't tell us who it was. Might be a loose end."

"The girl in question was a victim of drunk driving. She wrapped her car around a tree on her way home. Tragic," Bingham answered.

"But you said you wanted leverage. A live witness is more leverage than a dead one," Harper said.

Bingham drew a gun. "Harper, that girl goes into the hole alone or with you on top of her. Your choice."

Harper gulped. He stood tense, shoulders hunched. Then Bingham handed him a fresh roll of duct tape and he started to wrap it around the cooler. He took a cord of the same thin rope that had bound Mia Hill's hands and wrapped it around the chest, tying it with a fisherman's knot. Then he and Bingham were pushing the cooler, pushing it towards the edge of the landfill. They came to the lip and gave one final heave. The cooler tumbled out of sight. Down, down, down into the pit. Scott imagined he could hear it falling, rolling end over end, battering its cargo all the way.

Bingham left the edge of the frame, and reappeared driving a bulldozer which pushed a thick mound of trash down over the edge. Then another, and another. She was probably still alive as they buried her, Scott thought. Finally, Bingham left the cockpit and peered over the edge. Apparently, he considered his work done. He looked over at Harper. "Let's go," he said. "And don't forget the fucking camera."

Harper began to walk towards it. He bent down, picked up the camera, and for a moment the frame was filled with his face, his expression haunted and sick. Scott recognized it; it was the look that had been on his face the moment before he had shot himself. Mystery solved. Scott finally knew why Harper had killed himself.

The tape ended the second it was over, Amanda ran for the bathroom and vomited. Sunny looked close to doing the same. Even the normally glib Colin was pale and shaking, though some of that may have been due to the blood loss. Scott took off his glasses and ran his hand through his hair. He had seen worse things in his life. But not many.

The only one unaffected by it was Spence. "A little amateurish, but a good effort with an interesting *mise en scene*," he said. "On the whole I think it's rather sweet."

"Shut the fuck up," Colin growled.

The hit man just smiled at him. "Makes me look like a member of the Chamber of Commerce, don't it?" he remarked. "Somewhat ironic, given that I think Pike actually *is* a member of the Chamber of Commerce."

Colin turned from him, his hand to his mouth. "So what do we do with this?" he asked, his voice shaking.

There was the sound of running water and then Amanda appeared in the doorway looking a little worse for wear, but still strong enough to look disgusted. "What the fuck are you talking about? We use it to expose Pike"

"Did I miss something?" Colin said. "Because Pike's not actually on the tape."

"She names him."

"She names his son. Who, from what I heard, has recently taken a sabbatical, no doubt to some place from which extradition is a real bitch."

"You think he can get away from that clean?"

Colin shrugged. "Depends what you mean by clean. Will he still get invited to all the best parties? I doubt it. People will probably stop taking his money, or at least demand a few more middlemen between it and them. But will he be arrested? Will he end up in the Men's Colony? I don't think so. He'll just move down to Montecito and have his money console him there. Bingham Earle will go to jail. But I don't think you want to see this stop with Earle."

"The police, the D.A. whoever, will lean on Earle with this, get him to turn on Pike," Sunny said.

"That's one possibility. The other possibility is that Bingham's got a sweetheart somewhere, or an illegitimate kid who he would prefer not to see chopped up and fed to some pit bulls. Or maybe the D.A. and the police on the case will be the ones in Pike's pocket, and they'll put pressure on Bing to take the fall instead. Bing himself said it on the tape, Pike has leverage on everyone."

"Why don't you just tell us what you're suggesting?" Scott asked, taking off his glasses and rubbing his thumb and forefinger over the pressure points under his eyebrows.

"Hit him where it hurts," Colin said, spreading his hands. "Put a price tag on this thing that breaks his spine. Without money, the guy has no more pull. We can destroy him with this."

Amanda was looking at him like he had just crawled out from under something dark and wet. "I can't believe what you're saying."

Colin turned to her. "If you want a nice noble moral victory that leaves the perpetrator free, then feel free to stick to your plan. Personally, I want to see the fucker hurt."

"I don't know, man," Spence said. "That seems a little mercenary, even for me."

Colin turned to Scott. "Can I shut him up?"

Spence chose that moment to kick Colin in the kneecap. As he screamed and went down, Spence was on his feet. As Colin was on his knees trying to regain his balance, Spence raised his hands above his head and brought down his fists two-handed, like a club, into Colin's face. There was a loud crunch as his nose broke.

Spence pivoted. Luckily, the door was opened by a handle not a knob. Spence brought his hands down on it, but he lost his grip and the handle sprung back up. Spence turned. Sunny had recovered from the shock of Spence's actions before the others – he was rushing towards Spence from across the room at top speed. Spence idly wondered if he was about to get his ass beat by the same Korean for the third time in as many days.

He brought his hands down clumsily on the door handle again. The handle caught on his coat. He pulled, the door opened and Spence was free. He vaulted over the iron railing and landed on the flight of steps that led down to the parking lot. He bent his knees as he hit concrete and started to run as soon as he was sure of his footing. He was in the parking lot before the door opened again.

Sunny and Colin stood at the top of the staircase, looking down at him in disbelief. He guessed he hadn't broken the cocky one's knee. That was too bad. He wished he could take a moment to savor their astonishment, but there was no time for that. He took off down the block sprinting. The others followed; he could hear their footsteps on the steps behind him, and then echoing in the parking lot. But Sunny was fat and Colin was running a quart low of blood with a knee that, even if it wasn't broken, had to hurt like a bitch. He was confident about his ability to outpace them. After a few blocks Spence could no longer hear them, and when he finally dared to look behind him they weren't in sight.

Spence had just decided he was safe and that in a few hours he would go back to the motel, collect his car leave, San Rita in the rear-view permanently and just cut his losses, when the pickup truck roared around the corner and made a beeline for him. Spence briefly considered playing it cool, but there was no mistaking the truck's intentions. He didn't waste time wondering who these people might be, he just turned on his heels and ran – only to have a second late-model Ford come roaring down the deserted streets from the opposite direction, neatly cutting off his path.

Spence looked around – there were no bars in the area, and if there were any witnesses they were certainly making themselves inconspicuous. Before he could think any further, what felt suspiciously like a thick pine ax handle slammed into his kidneys with some force, driving him to his hands and knees. Spence locked his bound hands behind his head in a futile attempt to protect his skull and show he was unarmed. The ax handle was soon joined by a second, and the two beat a tattoo across his back and ribs in merry tandem. Unlike with Wan, Spence was not going to get away with just bruises.

After what felt like an eternity Spence felt two pairs of hands grab at his elbows and pull him to his feet. His head swam, but Spence was eventually able to recognize Bingham Earle regarding him with some satisfaction. He pulled back his arm and hit Spence across the face with a good left hook. Spence's head snapped back and he felt his nose go. "Break his jaw," he heard Bingham say. "That way we won't have to listen to him talk."

"Wait," Spence said.

"See what I mean?" replied Bingham, and he leaned back, apparently ready to do the job himself.

"If I can't talk there are all sorts of things you won't find out." Spence said. "Who I was just with, for example."

Bingham let his arm fall to his side. "I'm listening."

~ ~ ~

Sunny and Colin witnessed this from two blocks away, concealed behind the deep hedges that ran along one of the row houses.

"What should we do?" Sunny asked.

"Whad? Nodding." Colin said. He was clutching his face, trying not to breathe. The initial adrenaline of the chase had worn out and the pain in his nose was back like a motherfucker. It was tough to talk, but he managed, "Ond thind we know dey'll give the son of a bidch the ending he deserbes."

"Well what if he tells them about us?"

"Whyd would he? We're hid only-" Colin started, then faltered as the two thick men who had been beating on Spence shoved him in the backseat of the pickup truck. Bingham gave a high, sharp whistle and rolled his finger in the air, then got in the passenger seat of the first truck and sped off. The other followed.

"They're heading for the hotel!" Sunny shouted. Without another word the two of them started running.

~ ~ ~

Scott knew something was wrong. After spending so long in trouble, he felt as if he had developed a sixth sense for it. He could feel it coming the same way some old folks could feel the weather in their joints. He copied "Insurance" to Spence's desktop, then removed the disc from Spence's computer and handed it to Amanda.

"Put that in your purse," he said. "We need to get out of here."

They had just started for the door when the roar of engines from the parking lot filled the room. Scott turned and looked around. The room was so fucking small; there was nowhere to hide – only the bathroom, the main room and a small walk-in closet. It was a desperate hope but the only possible refuge. "Get in the closet," he said to Amanda.

"What? No, I'm not leaving you," she said.

"They can't do anything to me that hasn't already been done, can you say the same?" he asked. She looked him in the eyes, unwavering.

"You have a responsibility," he said. "You're the only one who has a chance of getting this information out there.

For Mia and God knows how many other girls who are rotting at the bottom of Pike's trash heap."

That did it. Scott could hear the boots on the steps. "Go!" he hissed. She went.

Scott went to the door – head them off here, he thought, keep them out of the room as much as possible, it was the girl's only hope. There was the crack of a body hitting the wooden door. Scott grabbed the laptop and went towards the door. He opened it just as the man on the other end started to bring his shoulder in for another swing. He checked himself and stumbled awkwardly, then looked up at Scott and raised his fist.

"There's no need for that," he said, holding up the laptop. "I have what you're looking for right here." Confused, the man looked over at his shoulder and down at Bingham Earle, who stood in the parking lot smoking a cigarette.

"Where's the disc?" Earle asked.

"No disc," Scott said. "Spence copied it to his computer."

"Bullshit."

"It's not."

"How many in there with you?"

"Just me."

"Spence said he met with 'people.' "

"Would that be the first time Spence lied to you?"

Bingham considered this. "Check the room," he commanded. The two men began to shove their way past Scott just as the sound of sirens rose still distant, but approaching.

"Shit," Bingham said. The two men muscled past Scott but contented themselves with a quick look under the bed and in the bathroom.

"No one's here," one of the guys called.

"Alright," Bingham said. He pointed at Scott. "But you're coming with us."

"The hell I am," Scott said.

"Wasn't asking." Bingham said, and one of the thugs grabbed Scott's arm and twisted it almost to the breaking point behind his back. He forced Scott forward down the steps, towards the open truck doors that seemed like a waiting maw. They fed him to it.

~ ~ ~

As Colin and Sunny arrived at the motel, they were just in time to watch the taillights of the two trucks recede in the distance towards the dark highways that would spirit them out of the city and into the country, into Pike's domain.

"Shid," said Colin. He spat out a mixture of blood and mucus and his voice was clearer. He sat down on the curb and clutched his knee, finally allowing himself to feel the pain from *that* wound. "That's it," he said. "That's fucking it."

They were quiet for a moment which was when they heard the sounds of distant sirens.

"We really should not be here." Colin said. Sunny reached out his arm and helped him to his feet. He winced as he put weight back on his leg. "Let's get out of here."

"Not yet," Sunny said. "We should check the room."

"Why? We just saw Bing's men clean it out. Best-case scenario, the cops that get here are clean and we have to explain whatever crazy shit's been reported to them. Worst-case scenario, they're dirty, they stick us in the back of their cruisers and drive us out to Pike's ranch."

Sunny shook his head. "Scott's smart, he may have left something behind."

"Like what?" Colin said. The door opened above them, and Amanda looked down at them.

"How?" Sunny asked.

"Scott distracted them. I still have the disc." The sounds of the sirens went up a notch in volume.

"As happy as I am to see you alive," Colin said, "Can we just get the fuck out of here?"

~ ~ ~

They sat around Sunny's kitchen table, their hands around steaming mugs of tea none of them felt like drinking. Alicia had waited up for them. Her face had fallen when she saw that Scott and the man who had come to kill her were missing. They had just finished recounting what they had seen in the motel room and what had happened afterward, and now settled into an uneasy silence as they realized they had no idea what to do.

Amanda broke the silence. "We'll put it in tomorrow's paper," she said firmly, "It might not take Pike all the way down, but even he won't be able to put the lid back on. Everyone will know him for what he is."

"And what about Scott?" Sunny asked. "We just let them kill him tonight? Chalk it up to collateral damage? Tough break, pal?"

"Scott was a big boy," Colin said. "He did what he set out to accomplish, and as much as I hate to say this, he's probably already dead. Bastard probably went out with a smile on his face, knowing he successfully lobbed a grenade right into their safe house before he went."

"The Scott I knew wasn't one for grand gestures," Sunny said.

"Maybe not," Amanda said quietly. "But he made one. He sacrificed himself so this information would get out. We have to honor that."

"Boy, those Catholic schools sure taught you how to love a martyr," Sunny said. They both looked up at him, shocked. "Maybe Scott was willing to sacrifice himself in order to break this story. I, for one, would prefer that he didn't have to."

Colin had recovered somewhat. "Well I, for one, would prefer I was married to Mila Kunis and had a Stingray in my garage, but it's just not going to happen."

Sunny looked around his homey kitchen, sighed then shot Colin a look. "Are you telling me, Mr. Connected, that you don't have the number of some lowlife on Pike's crew?"

"I might," Colin allowed. "But what would you do with it?"

Sunny smiled. "I'll talk to the big man and make a deal."

~ ~ ~

They had kept Scott on the floor the whole ride out. Realistically, Scott knew the trip to Pike's ranch couldn't be much over twenty minutes. But underneath the boots of two thick-necked thugs on his way to what might possibly be his death, it felt much longer.

The smooth pavement gave way to rough dirt. The car rocked and swayed as it turned its way up switchbacks and around thick curves. They went for a long time up a steep grade, then they started down. The smell of cow shit and animal stink filled the truck. They weren't headed anywhere good.

Finally, the truck came to a stop. The two men jerked Scott off the floor while Bingham walked around from the driver's side. They were in front of a barn that was flanked by a cattle pen. The barn cast its hulking shape against the sky, its darkness broken only by a thin line of light, like a streak of white paint, where someone had left the big steel doors ajar. The light coming from it was white and fluorescent; it looked sickly and demented. On the whole, Scott would rather be out here in the dark. But the men who flanked him had begun to drag him towards the door, so apparently that was not in the cards.

After being joined by their numbers in the trucks, about a dozen men now milled around the yard. They smoked, spat, and talked in low, furtive voices. None of them looked at Scott as he was dragged past, as if by some improbability he managed to be just outside of each one's peripheral vision. Scott thought he recognized some of them, but in the dim light it was hard to be sure.

A few of the men had dogs near them, pit bulls, Rottweilers, and a few ranch dogs of indeterminate mongrel breed which had been threaded through decades of selection with the meanest of stock. Most of them paid no attention to Scott. A few got to their feet and growled at him, but their minders pulled at their leashes and quieted them. I guess that proves I am visible after all, Scott mused.

They were before the doors. Two men walked past the men holding Scott and pulled the barn doors open, bathing him in a light that made him flinch. When he was dragged inside and saw what was waiting for him, he flinched again.

The floor of the barn was concrete and slightly concave, with a drain in the center. Chains and hooks hung from the ceiling. It was a killing floor.

In the center of the room a sheet of plastic had been rolled out and a metal folding chair placed in the center. Spence sat in the chair, his hands bound behind him with barbed wire. Dark blood dripped from his wrists, where it blended with the impressive amount of blood that already coated the plastic. Three-gallon bottles of bleach sat at the edge of the tarp. All three were open, and the cauterizing smell of the bleach wafted and blended with the coppery scent of the blood.

He couldn't have been delivered more than five minutes ahead of me, Scott marveled.

A man stood in front of Spence in a white butcher's smock that had already been dyed half red, holding a carving knife slick with blood. It took Scott a moment to recognize him as Pike. He looked awfully different from when he posed for 4-H pictures.

Pike looked up from his work. Spence looked over his shoulder, his face swollen and battered.

Pike pointed at Scott with the knife. "You're that rummy reporter." Scott saw no reason to deny it, and nodded. Pike gave a short bark of a laugh and shook his head. "Boy, did you pick the wrong time to find your scruples."

Scott's throat was dry. He was scared shitless, but he managed to reply: "I guess that all depends on how you look at it."

Pike nodded as if allowing the point. "It's not too late for you to lose them again."

Scott deeply wished he had a cigarette. "Do you really expect me to believe that?"

Pike shrugged. "It comforts some men, but I can see you're someone who likes to take things straight. I admire that. If it makes you feel better, I'll make things quick. Not like for this smart bastard here," he said, with a jerk of his head towards Spence. "You were just doing your job. Got nothing against that."

Scott closed his eyes, but only for a moment. He hoped Pike mistook it for a blink. So this was where he cashed in his chips. Well, that was all right. He had always known that what had happened thirty years ago had been a temporary stay of execution, not an acquittal. He owed the world a violent death, and now the world had come to collect. He had been given the time to do one last thing that was worth a damn, and for that he was thankful, even though he no longer held anyone or anything in his heart to be thankful to.

He had passed the torch on to the right people they would know what to do. He had always been a man who paid what he owed. Now the time had come for him to pay in full.

His contemplation was interrupted by the sound of blood and bone hitting the floor. Spence had let go of a long mouthful of blood and a tooth had come with it. He was turned, craning his head in his seat as far as it could go. The eye that was visible was swollen almost shut, that entire half of his face a large bruise marbled purple and black. Incredibly, the man was smiling. "Alright, so I know Scott's here. Does that mean Bing has arrived too?"

His question echoed off the high ceilings of the barn. It went unanswered. Spence's smile faltered in mock hurt. "I never took you for a discourteous man, Pike. You should answer your guest's question." Pike turned to Bing, who was standing by the door.

"Yeah, he's here."

"Gooood." Spence said, and then stopped for a moment to give a hacking cough and a wince of pain. "That pulled a doozy on the old ribs," he said. "Let me ask you then, Pike. You ever see this video you've killed so many people over?" Bing started to push towards Spence, but Pike held up an arm to stop him.

"No, I have not," Pike allowed.

"I thought not." Spence crowed. "Bing probably told you that it was Harp who made the tape, but judging from the video I'm guessing you must have been surprised a dumb good old boy like Harper had the wherewithal to be so forward-thinking. Am I right? Seemed much more like something crafty old Bing would do, didn't it?"

Bing was trying to muscle past Pike now, his face red, the veins and tendons in his neck sticking out like filled hoses. "That's a fucking lie!" he shouted. Spence started to laugh, which set off another coughing fit and another mouthful of blood splattering on the floor.

"Don't take my word for it," he said when he'd recovered. Pike was staring at Bing with eyes that had all the warmth of stone. "Ask the reporter if it's true. Mr. Objective Fourth Estate has seen it. He's got no reason to back me up. Hell, I tried to kill his protégé tonight, he's got no fondness for me whatsoever."

Pike turned to Scott, "Is this true?" he asked. Scott nodded.

Before Bing even had the chance to protest his innocence one more time, Pike backhanded him viciously across the face. The echo of the slap bounced off the high metal ceiling and cement floor, before being stamped out by Bing's cry. Unthinkingly, his hands shot up to his struck face, leaving his belly exposed.

Pike sunk his blade into it. It went in deep, with just a quarter of the blade visible, gleaming above the handle. Then he tore. Bing's screaming stopped and became a choking gag as he was laid open. He looked down at himself and clutched weakly for Pike's wrist, missed and gripped the exposed blade of the knife instead. Bing's eyes had gone glazed. Blood poured from his hand, but it was doubtful he felt it. Pike drew back the knife further, slicing open Bing's palm. One of his fingers came away with the pull as well, but Scott was unable to tell which one.

Pike began to wipe the blood off on his apron, Bing clutching at the air in front of him before his knees buckled and he fell straight on his ass, giving a little "Whoop" of surprise at the impact. Scott could see the pink of one of his intestines. He sat like that, looking up at the lights with glazed confusion as he tried to hold his insides inside him. He stayed like that until Pike whistled.

The doors slid open and two of the dogs that Pike had seen came barreling in at a run. There was plenty of blood in the air, and for a moment they hesitated between the man on the floor and the man in the chair. But the scent from Bing must have been stronger, because then they were on him.

This brought Bing back to something like full consciousness. His glassy eyes cleared and he started to scream. He beat at the dogs with frantic, flailing open-handed blows that bounced weakly off the dogs' hide. There was a snarl – Scott had just enough time to see one of the dogs sink its teeth into Bing's exposed entrails and begin to tug before he looked away. It took much longer for Bing to stop screaming than Scott thought it would.

When they had finished, Pike whistled again and the two handlers called for their dogs, who left what remained of Bing, licking their chops. Pike pointed his knife at Spence, who had also watched the whole thing, with an air of satisfaction that rivaled that of the dogs. "I was saving that for you," he said. "But don't get too comfortable. I'll find some other way for you to go."

He turned to Scott. "You didn't throw up." Scott shook his head. "Most men would have. I guess there's more to you than I thought." Pike concluded. "If I had known I would have had you on my payroll long ago."

"No, you wouldn't have," Scott replied. He was sure that at any moment Pike would lunge for him with that knife. He would only have a moment, if that.

"Still, it is a shame," Pike began, the blade twitched in his hand like a living thing, a falcon begging for its handler to unleash it. Scott steeled himself for a fight, for the end. Then the door opened again, this time unbidden.

Standing in the sickly light was someone Scott recognized very well. Karl Winslow looked down at what was left of Bingham Earle, and was not able to disguise the face of a man whose stomach has just lurched. Still, Scott figured the kid was one of the few here who could legitimately claim to have seen worse. He didn't know that Winslow was running with Pike. He idly wondered how long he had been. Still, he shouldn't have been surprised. Karl was just the kind of man Pike targeted: poor, tough, someone who ran on instinct rather than logic. Someone who didn't exactly have a lot of opportunities going for him.

Scott suddenly felt very sorry for Karl; the kid had sold his soul and didn't even know it yet. Perhaps, looking down at Bingham Earle, he knew it now. And for what? A nicer pickup truck? The wages of sin from a man like Pike were awful miserly.

Karl looked at Scott, then looked away, unable to meet his eyes. "There's a call for you, sir," he said.

Pike sighed. "Son, I know you're bright, so doesn't it seem to you that I might be otherwise occupied?"

"Ah yes, sir," he said. "But the thing is that I'm pretty sure it's important. It came in on Hitch's phone, and er, I guess you'd better hear it for yourself." Pike's eyes narrowed. He cast one last look at Scott and headed for the door. Karl held it open for him. He was just turning to go when Scott spoke his name.

Karl looked up at him, seeming genuinely pained. "I'm sorry, Mr. Molina, but there's nothing I can do for you. I didn't know they'd be bringing you up here, and I wouldn't have come if I did. But whatever jackpot you got yourself in I can't help you out of. You understand?"

"I understand," Scott said. "But you're wrong. There is something you can do for me." Karl looked at him doubtfully. "I just need a light," he said. He reached into his coat pocket and drew a cigarette. "Bing left me my cigarettes and took my lighter. Guess he didn't want me to pull a MacGuyver. Think you could give me a light?"

Karl face broke with something that looked like relief. Scott was giving him a chance to do something decent, even if it was a small thing. Karl would not get many more chances if he stayed with Pike.

He produced a Bic. Scott took it and lit his cigarette. He handed it back to Karl, who began to reach for it, then hesitated. "Go ahead and keep it, Mr. Molina," he said.

"You're sure?" Scott asked.

"Yeah. Everyone out there has got one, won't be a big deal."

"Thanks, Karl," Scott said. Karl nodded, and then turned away to walk out the door. The steel doors closed, and Scott heard the sound of a bolt closing. Karl wasn't going to go that far. That was alright. A doorway leading to twelve armed men wasn't much of an opportunity. Scott took a long drag and then walked around to consider the killer.

He was a mess. His clothing was torn and soaked with blood. His face was swollen, only one eye looking up at Scott, staring. Pike had been playing at him, carving long shallow cuts up and down his arms legs and torso.

"Isn't as frightful as it looks," Spence said, as if reading his mind, though Scott supposed in these circumstances that wasn't so hard. "Shallow cuts bleed more. That's why he's done it that way. There's been no permanent damage yet." Scott nodded. He didn't think a little permanent damage would be such a bad thing for this man. Spence nodded at the cigarette. "Can I have a drag?"

Scott considered the man's blood-caked lips. "All things considered, I'd rather just give you one." He pulled out his pack and lit a cigarette with Karl's lighter. He held it up for Spence, who took a few grateful drags in silence.

"I don't expect it to mean much," Spence said. "But I am sorry about trying to kill you and your boy. Wasn't anything personal, I was just trying to cover my tracks." Scott nodded; the exchange was no less surreal than the rest of his day. "That's enough," Spence said, and Scott flicked away the butt, which sizzled out in a pool of blood. Whether the blood was Spence's or Bing's was hard to tell.

"There's a pair of bolt cutters on the table next to me," Spence said, sounding oddly casual, just delivering a bit of FYI. "I know because Pike told me he was going to cut off my fingers and toes and feed them to me. I did get that man's dander up."

Scott said nothing, just took another drag.

"I don't suppose I could trouble you to use those to cut through the wire he's got me tied up with."

"That wouldn't seem very wise on my part," Scott said.

Spence tried to shrug, "Trust me, I am much more annoyed with them at this moment than I am with you."

"Why should I?" Scott retorted.

"Because if you let me free I'm going to kill as many of those men as I can. The more of them who die, the better chance you have of getting out of this."

Scott considered this and saw the truth in it. "You don't look like you're in much condition to thin the ranks."

That shrug again. "Some is better than none."

"What happens after?"

"After is after. I think for both of us the present is the more pressing concern. If there is an after, it'll be a bonus. But I think our time grows short."

"Two conditions," Scott said. "One, try not to kill the boy who was just in here. I know you saw him. His daddy is a friend of mine. Second, if there is an after it concerns me and you. Not me, you and the others. I let you go, they are out of your factoring."

"Done," Spence said.

There were so many implements on the table that it was hard to spot the bolt cutters, but he soon picked out their blue handles. He knelt down before Spence and began to free his legs. The wire consisted of three separate pieces, and it had been wrapped around tightly. The blood that flowed from the wounds it had made had partially dried, dying Spence's legs and forearms a dark black. Each time he snipped one of the strands a wave of vibration went up the strands, causing Spence to wince and draw in his breath in pain. Finally it was done, though the wire still stuck to Spence, the barbs dug into his flesh. Scott went around to the other side and began to work on his arms. The wire was wrapped tighter here, but there was less of it. Soon he was free.

Spence dug the wire out of his flesh, releasing fresh spurts of blood but kept his silence. Finally, the wire lay in a little pile at his feet. He stood up, shaky at first but ultimately steady. He rubbed at his wrists, unable to keep the pain off his face. Then he looked up at Scott and met his eyes for the first time since they had spoken.

For a moment neither man knew what would happen.

~ ~ ~

Pike stood in the dusty driveway in front of the barn. His men had backed up, making a little half circle around him. "Well?" Pike asked. "Anyone want to tell me what was so Goddamned important?" Finnigan, the large bodyguard with a shaved head, potato face and a big slab of beer gut, moved forward with a cell phone in his outstretched hand, trying to keep as much distance between himself and Pike as possible without being obvious. Pike snatched the cell phone out of his hand.

"Hello?"

"Has anything happened to Scott?" the voice on the other end asked. It was a young man's voice that Pike didn't recognize.

"Who is this?"

"It doesn't matter, you twisted old fuck. Now answer my question."

"Answer mine, or else I hang up the phone and get about my business."

"I'm the man who has the tape."

Pike closed his eyes; his grip on the phone grew so tight that his knuckles went white. He wished he could kill Bingham again – he'd find something worse for the bastard.

"That's impossible," Pike said.

"Willing to bet your life on that?"

"Boy, I would advise you to run and leave the state, but in truth it wouldn't do you any good. I don't let anyone fuck with me this way, and I'll hunt you and whoever you love down no matter where you go."

"Unless I end up in San Quentin, I think I'll be outside your sphere of influence."

"Willing to bet your life on that?"

"I'm willing to bet that you'll take your last chance at containment. You have exactly one more shot to keep this under control."

"And what chance is that?"

"Even exchange. Scott for the tape."

"Well, if that's a deal you feel you can make, you just come on up to the ranch. But I wouldn't wait too long. I might grow impatient."

With that, he hung up the phone, looked at the number that had just called and wrote it down. He handed the phone back to its owner and looked around. It took him a second to realize he was looking for Bing. He would need a new lieutenant soon, before this became too annoying. He turned to a kid he recognized, whose name he almost knew.

"Find out whose number that was," he said. "If they haven't arrived by dawn we'll just be obliged to go to them."

~ ~ ~

Sunny hung up the phone. Colin, Amanda and Alicia were both looking up at him expectantly.

147

"What did he say?" Amanda asked.

"He said to come and get him," Sunny replied.

"Was that come and get him as in 'Oh sure, drop by and pick him up,' or come and get him as in, 'I dare you to try and come and get him?' " Colin asked.

"That's open to interpretation," Sunny said.

"Shit," groaned Alicia.

"Well what are we going to do?" Amanda asked.

Sunny sighed, "I suppose I'm going to go and get him."

There was a long silence around the table, which Colin finally broke. "Are you sure that's ... wise?" He asked.

"Probably not, but I don't see what else I can do. Can I borrow one of your guns?"

"Do you know how to use a gun?"

"No."

"I suppose I'll have to go with you, then." Colin's face was battered. Alicia had helped him tape his nose, and he had worked out a splint for his left knee. He now stood a little shakily but was basically steady.

"Thank you."

"I'm going too." Amanda said.

"I only have two guns," Colin said.

"That's alright. I still want to see this through to end."

"I'll go too," Alicia said.

"No," said Sunny.

"Honey, if you think I'm letting you go off on your own to let yourself get killed, you're fucking crazy."

"If it all does go wrong," Sunny said, "we need someone who knows what's going on safe and sound to deliver that video. This goes beyond us. Frankly, we don't have the right to risk it not getting out. If it's not Amanda, it has to be you."

A long silence followed. Sunny could not quite bring himself to meet her eyes. He told himself that it wasn't a betrayal.

The silence was broken by the sound of metal sliding against the table. Colin pushed a semi-automatic towards Sunny. He held the magazine in his hand.

"It's simple, really." He pointed a small button on the side of the pistol. "That's the safety. When you're not ready to use it, make damn sure it's on. When you're ready to use it, make damn sure it's off. Other than that, just point and pull. Now go ahead and show me that you know the difference."

Sunny picked up the gun. It was much heavier than he thought it was going to be.

~ ~ ~

They piled into Sunny's car and Colin directed them to where they were going. Pike owned several stretches of land in the city and around it, but when Colin spoke of "the ranch" it could only mean the grouping of acres to the east of the city, past his vineyards. It was the heart of his fiefdom, the place where his autonomy was not questioned – where he brokered his deals, held his political fundraisers and his charity Santa Maria-style barbecues. The cops did not come out unless they were invited.

They had left Alicia with the laptop and instructions on what to do with the file if they did not return by the time the sun came up: She'd upload it to the Internet first, and then deliver a copy to Russell and tell him what had happened.

They were betting on Russell not being in Pike's pocket, which seemed reasonable. But even so, they wouldn't make him the only one to hold the power. They had burned a copy of the disc to show to Pike and to destroy if necessary. Sunny didn't know if it would fool him; he couldn't help but doubt it. But it would get them in the door, give them a fool's chance of their plan working. He, Colin and Amanda had sketched it out quickly. How workable it was, Sunny didn't know. But he supposed he was about to find out.

He and Alicia had managed never to quite meet each other's eyes during that last half hour, even when they had held each other briefly in the doorway. He knew he was hurting her, and he hated himself for it. She didn't understand, and that was fair, because neither did he. He only knew that if he left Scott to his fate, even if everything else went off without a hitch, even if he walked into the Telegraph's office tomorrow and brought the whole of Pike's rotten empire crashing down on top of him and crushed him under its weight, it would be the hollowest of victories. He would never really be able to look himself in the mirror again. There was no real choice at all. He simply felt compelled.

They cut through the night, the radio tuned to KPIG. Brad Paisely sang about never leaving Harlan alive. Colin snorted and reached to turn it off, but Amanda asked him quietly to leave it on. He let his hand drop away, and the eerie song finished as they approached Pike's ranch.

About half a mile from the place where the county road became Pike's private drive, they pulled over to the side of the road. Colin began to get out of the car, then paused. "Remember," he said in a low tone, pointing at his knee. "I'm moving slower than you are. So give me a bit of a head start." Sunny nodded, Colin nodded back, then he turned to Amanda. He seemed on the verge of saying something, but decided against it and left the car. Amanda turned and watched as he loped off into the darkness.

"Sorry I dragged you into this," Sunny said to her. "Scott wanted to keep you out and I should have listened to him."

Amanda gave a scoffing laugh. "You guys still don't get it. I could have bailed out any time I wanted. I'm here because I chose to be. Same as you. This matters and I'm happy I'm here. Don't try and take that away from me."

"Happy?" Sunny asked with a grin.

"Well, as one can be under the circumstances." She said.

"Well in that case, I'm glad you're with us," Sunny said. Amanda nodded but didn't say anything. They sat for a few minutes in the country dark until she spoke again.

"Do you think he's had enough time?" It wasn't really a question. It was time to face what the night held. Sunny nodded and got out of the car. He waited for Amanda to do the same. They began to walk towards the gate to Pike's ranch.

~ ~ ~

Amanda couldn't quite put into words why she was coming, why she was risking so much. There were safer ways to do this, but they would all leave Scott dead and Pike with the chance to slip his noose, and she couldn't have that.

Because this was what she had always said she, wanted wasn't it? The chance to confront the powerful and the evil? Well, Pike was about as powerful and evil as they came. He was entrenched like a tick, sucking out the blood from her home for his own unspeakable, unthinkable wants, while injecting it at the same time with God knew what kind of disease and sickness.

Now that she had her chance to confront evil, would she prove herself a coward? One of those people who talked big and said all the right things about justice, but when it came down to it, wasn't willing to risk anything? Who would turn their head so they would be left alone? She thought not. She was walking right into the heart of darkness in her little town, and she was doing it with her eyes open.

She thought of the stories the priests had taught her. About Daniel untouched in the den of the lions, and Shadrach, Meshach and Abednego unconsumed by the flames of the oven. Of course, she didn't believe God would save her as she willingly walked into the hands of her enemies. It was much more par for the course for God to allow his servants to come to bad ends – to end up like the Macabees, with their limbs hacked off and their eyes and tongues torn out of their living heads. Even Christ had said depending on God to save you from danger was not a safe bet, when Satan advised him to take a flying leap off the temple wall.

But even as a child she had understood that the point of these stories was not that you would be protected from physical harm, but that at the end of the day it was truly better to put yourself in danger for something that was truly important than to live in corrupt safety, – that even if you died, a part of you that was greater than your body would be protected.

And after all the doubt and dogma, Amanda still truly believed that – that there were things not merely worth putting your life on the line for, but even more important than that. Things that if you didn't put your life on the line for, you would find that afterward your life would be worth a little less. Sunny could make all the cracks about martyrs that he wanted. As far as Amanda was concerned, there were far worse things to be called.

She was making sure tonight that "coward" would never be one of them.

~ ~ ~

Colin limped through the wilderness about a quarter mile from the road, just keeping it in sight. The land out here was scrub – all dry grass, cow shit and low brush and bushes. Not a lot of cover to be had. Colin would have to count on the darkness to keep him hidden.

He reached a barbed wire fence that marked the edge of Pike's property. The wire was old, loose and rusty – there only for appearances and not much else. Anyone who made his way out here wouldn't be stupid enough to go onto Pike's land without an invitation. Colin easily ducked between two strands.

Every step he took sent a wave of pain up and down his leg from the epicenter of his knee. It was like having an electric jolt shock him on each stride. Colin would have killed for an ice pack. He had managed to hide how badly he was hurting from the others by taping it up himself, but he could only hope things went smoothly – though he knew that was being optimistic to the point of stupidity. His knee had swollen up to the size of a grapefruit. If he had to run ... well, that did not even bear thinking about.

A little hill rose to his right, blocking his view of the road. He crept towards it, crouched down, keeping low to the ground, his knee sending a shriek of protest as he did. When he reached the crest he lay on the ground, peering at the road below.

There, before a wide wrought-iron gate with a cattle catcher on either side, stood two men. They leaned against the gate, smoking and talking to each other in low tones Colin could not make out. One gave a rueful chuckle and shoved the other. Colin could just make out the sound of gravel under shoes; he heard it before the two guards did. Then again, he was expecting it. Sunny and Amanda were coming.

The two emerged from the night and the guards finally caught sight of them. Colin drew his gun and propped his elbows on the ground. He hit the safety. It was doubtful he could hit them from this far off, but at the very least he'd distract them, get them to shoot off into the darkness. Maybe even just go for cover. Hopefully it wouldn't come to that. Colin might not be as attached as Sunny, but he'd rather see Scott alive than dead.

The guards were spooked. They drew their guns and started walking towards the pair with careful, shuffling steps. Sunny and Amanda had their hands up. This was the first test. They had taped Sunny's gun to his ankle; if they searched him they would find it. He had to hope they wouldn't search him.

One of the guards picked up a walkie-talkie from the gatepost while the other kept his gun on Sunny and Amanda. Colin caught a quick burst of static, but he was too far away to hear the rest of it. It was possible that Pike would just order these men to shoot them where they stood. Possible, but Colin didn't think it likely. This place was like a Venus flytrap – the deeper you let them walk in the harder it was for them to get out.

Pike had apparently come to the same conclusion. The guard put down the walkie-talkie and motioned them forward. They dropped their hands to their sides. Colin gave a little sigh of relief, put the safety back on and holstered his gun.

He could see a pickup truck about a hundred yards up the road. He moved back from the road, down to the bottom of the little rise he had been on, and crept his way up Pike's land. He hadn't gotten very far before he heard the sound of the pickup's engine. He risked moving closer to the road and watched as the taillights crested a steep hill and then reappeared much smaller about a quarter mile down the road.

The road forked about a mile past there, the right path leading up the rise to Pike's big house, where he occasionally played host with wine from his vineyard, treating everyone to his view. The left led deeper into a ranch past a deep copse of trees that hid what went on there from the sight of the gentry. It was where the work got done, Pike's was no hobby ranch, and that was where the work would be done tonight. The truck went down the left-hand path.

Colin began to move a little quicker, less worried about noise and visibility now that the guards had moved ahead. He doubted that there were any men on Pike's ranch that weren't immediately at hand. Everyone had gathered at the killing grounds. It was time for Colin to get there too.

~ ~ ~

Karl gave a heavy sigh and dug for another cigarette. He had to adjust the shotgun into the crook of his arm. It wasn't his; they had given it to him when he arrived. Karl didn't like the gun, but didn't say so. The truth was that he didn't have much experience with shotguns. They were a weapon for rednecks, beginners and hunters, and Karl was none of the above. In the service he had used rifles. The very few times he had picked up a firearm since being back home they had been pistols his buddies had taken out to the gun range.

He was glad he had come out here with a full pack. He had already gone through half of it. Plus, he didn't know these guys well enough to bum, and anyway that wasn't the first impression you wanted to make on a crew you'd be working with: a moocher who didn't come prepared with his gear. He was nervous, there was no way to hide it. No reason to, either. Back overseas, some of the guys would get all macho, get pissed enough to slam your head through a wall if you even suggested they were frightened, but Karl had always felt that you had to be in touch with the fear. It would give you the edge, keep you alive. Ignoring it was stupid, like ignoring asthma.

But seeing Scott like that, that had been some feeling other than nervousness. Karl didn't suppose the old man would be walking out of that barn alive. That was a shame, it really was; Karl had always liked the old guy. But it wasn't exactly sadness that Karl felt, just the same resignation that had haunted Karl since approximately his second week in Iraqi.

Scott had bought his ticket; now he was taking the ride. Didn't mean it was right, just that Scott had chosen his course of action and now he was reaping what he'd sown. In a perfect world Scott would be alive and Karl's employer would be dead. Hell, Scott deserved to live and Pike deserved to die. But this world was not perfect. Karl had seen more than enough evidence to convince him of this. In this world there was little that factored in less than who deserved what.

When an IED blew at the side of the road and thanks to the prevailing winds the guy on your left got a face full of shrapnel and the guy on your right had his nose blown clean off, was it because either of them deserved what they got? When Karl's platoon was on patrol and Haji drew a bead on the guy next to him instead of Karl, was it because Karl was somehow deserving of protection? Did these dead men share some secret sin that Karl was innocent of? Hell no. They had all drank alcohol from the same bottles of mouthwash, all jerked off to the same old issues of Maxim, all passed around the same bootleg copies of *Hostel*. There was no sense to it at all.

The only comfort you could take, the only order you could find, was the fact that they had all chosen the path that had led them to that place. What happened at those crucial moments of time, like clearings on the path, they had no say over, but getting there they had their say. Karl used to think that what happened there was up to God. Now he thought that whatever happened there just happened at the spur of the moment. If there was a God, Karl couldn't help but picture him like Two-Face in the Batman comics he used to read as a kid, grinning his leering, distended grin as he flipped his coin. No grand design, just the instant, deciding who would receive grace and who would be lost with little thought and no kindness.

Scott may not deserve what was coming to him. But he had walked the path to get it. Now what would come to him was not any business of anybody's, with the possible exception of the grinning God with his coin.

Karl was stirred from his reverie by the arrival of a pickup truck. It stopped a few yards outside the gravel circle. Pike pushed his way towards it, eager like an angry dog at the end of its tether who finds that the thing he wants to sink its teeth into has just been dumb enough to wander into its yard.

The car left its lights on and two men Karl didn't know emerged. They reached into the back, drew up the seats and brought two people blinking into the headlights. Karl stopped, his jaw hanging open. Scott he could handle, but not this. Not the one person who had always been there to test his theories.

~ ~ ~

"Do you even know why we're here?" Amanda asked. They were the first words she had spoken since they had gone into the back of the pickup truck. At first the two men had come on strong and Sunny was pretty sure he had made a terrible mistake, that this rescue mission would end with them dead by the side of the road before it even began. But then one had called up Pike, and he and Amanda had been herded into the back of the truck. Now they drove in silence, and Sunny still could not help but wonder if they had made a terrible mistake.

"Shut the fuck up," the man in the passenger seat snarled without turning around. They were nervous and inexperienced. Sunny hadn't realized just how young they might be. The one in the passenger seat might not even be twenty yet. Just kids. That didn't make them any safer.

Kids could be as stupid as anyone and a good deal stupider than most. It could play to their advantage. Sunny still had the gun, cold and heavy against his leg. Or it could end up getting them killed in the long run. These kids could get spooked easier than veterans could, and Sunny knew from experience that when kids with guns got scared, bad things happened.

The kids drove quickly down the dirt roads. The suspension bounced and rocked; every quick turn nearly threw Sunny into the wall. Sunny could only pray that no deer or livestock crossed their path. At this clip even a stray coyote would be trouble – they'd be dead before Pike got a chance to kill him. Below the sight line of the men in the front, he and Amanda clutched hands.

They drove through a thick grove of eucalyptus trees, their scent heavy enough to overpower the smell of sawdust, fast food and chaw that filled the cab of the truck. Sunny loved the eucalyptuses and their smell – they grew everywhere here. Every park, every neighborhood, every open space that could support them did. He sometimes wondered if that was why he hadn't ended up settling here. The smell followed him wherever he went. He closed his eyes and drew it in. For all he knew this was the last moment in his life that would belong to him.

A little less than a mile up ahead he could see the faint white glow of what looked like sodium lights. Soon the truck bounced around a corner and came to a clearing. At the far end of it, two metal poles stretched up into the sky. A ring of sodium lights topped each, making it look like two halos floated above. Between them lay a large steel barn and a small corral, in front of which stood Pike and about ten men. Pike was clear in the lights of the truck, but the men behind him milled about in the shadows. They remained dark shapes, as faceless and indistinct as ghosts.

The guards left the lights on and got out of the front of the cab, pulling back the seat and herding Amanda and Sunny out. Pike stood unblinking in the truck's lights. Sunny couldn't help but think it was a bad sign that Pike had not bothered to change out of his blood-soaked clothes.

Sunny had never seen Pike outside of the pictures his paper occasionally printed. Where he tended to blend together with whatever well-to-do group of white people he was posing with. But standing in his presence, he realized there was something different about him. He would have been intimidating even if he hadn't been dressed in a butcher's apron covered in blood. Sunny knew Pike was in his sixties, but he had the build of a man twenty years younger. Tall, probably just a hair under six feet, with broad shoulders and thick, well-muscled arms that showed clearly in the tight white clothes he was wearing. His mustache was white but thick. But it was his eyes, steady and unblinking, that made Sunny truly worried. The rest of Pike looked as though he had just crawled out of hell, but his eyes were steady and calm. Had he seen just a touch of madness there he might have thought they had a chance. As it was, it looked as though Pike were just spending another day at the office.

"The disc," he said, and held out a hand palm-up. The hand was gloved and the glove was slick and red with blood.

"Where's Scott?" Sunny asked.

"He's in there," Pike said, jerking his head over his shoulder.

"Doesn't look like you've kept your end of it," Sunny said.

Pike looked down at himself. "None of this blood is his," he responded.

"I want to see him," Sunny said.

"I want to see the disc," Pike replied.

Sunny turned to Amanda, who reached into her purse and pulled out the disc they had burned. The jewel case it was in caught the light of the truck. Pike took it from her hand. As he considered it, he spoke.

"Now, son, I want you to think real carefully," he said. "This is the last copy of this God-forsaken video that there is?" Sunny nodded. "You're sure now?" Pike said. "Because let me tell you, I have heard that one before."

"It's the last," Sunny said.

Pike spoke as he looked at the disc, twisting it in the light like a jeweler looking for flaws. "Because I went ahead and got your address using my reverse telephone directory, Mr. Wan. I know where you live, and should I have any reason to suspect that this is not the last copy of Bingham's tape, I'm going to go to your house and kill anyone who happens to be there." With that he abruptly met Sunny's eyes, as if to catch a lie there by surprise. "Now," he said, "Knowing the risks, are you absolutely sure that you're telling me the truth?"

Sunny met his gaze. He didn't blink. "I'm sure," he said.

Pike considered this for a minute more, and then he whistled. Three men brandishing guns stepped out of the darkness and into the light. They pointed their guns at Sunny and Amanda, who both raised their hands. "What the fuck?!" Sunny said.

"I'm just doing what you asked," Pike said. He was wearing a folksy grin now. "We're going to go see Scott now. I just don't want you to get lost along the way."

Sunny struggled not to look behind him into the darkness, where Colin was supposed to be waiting if something like this were to happen. Where the fuck was he? Sunny knew the gimp leg would keep him, but he should have been able to catch up by now. He had to buy more time.

Surprisingly, it was Amanda who spoke. "Karl?" she asked. One of the men, one of the older ones, about Sunny's age and holding a sawed-off shotgun, stopped and looked uneasy. "Karl, what are you doing here with these men?" Amanda asked.

Sunny could see that Karl actually blushed in the low light, like a guy who'd been called out by his girlfriend in the company of his boys. "It's nothing personal," he said. "I didn't know it was you they'd be bringing out."

"Karl, do you know what these men do?"

"We didn't all get to go to Harvard, Amanda," Karl replied. He looked away when he said it, unable to meet Amanda's eye, "Some of us have to step outside the law to get what's ours. Make our own way." His voice sounded a bit steadier during that last part. Sunny judged that it had been running around his head for the better part of the night and he was pleased to have the chance to say it out loud.

"They rape women, Karl. They kill innocent people. Karl, this isn't about legal and illegal. This is about good and evil." Amanda said, "I know you know the difference. You are not of this."

"Hey," Pike's voice cut in. He was halfway across the gravel yard, having apparently missed what was being said. "I didn't ask you all to converse with them, bring them to the barn."

"What's he going to do to me in that barn, Karl? Are you going to watch?" Amanda asked. "Are you going to take your turn?" Karl had to look away again.

Pike whistled, and one of the others jabbed Sunny in the ribs with his rifle. "Get moving," he said. Sunny did, trudging through the gravel, the sound somehow magnified in the night air. The barn waited before him.

Pike was walking towards it, but he was still about twenty yards out. Two men moved in front of him. One unfastened a bolt and drew back the doors.

That was when the screaming started.

~ ~ ~

It was the second man who screamed. The first man had gotten a cleaver in his neck that had gone in so deep it had lodged in the man's spine. His vocal cords and windpipe had been severed before he had even made a sound.

Spence had stood by the door with the cleaver in hand pulled back tense and waiting. They had waited so long that Scott was worried that when the men did come for them, Spence would be caught off guard, the way you could be when a long red light finally turns to green. He needn't have worried. The moment the doors began to move, Spence struck like a coiled snake and embedded his fangs.

As the first man fell silently, Spence reached for the gun at his belt, ignoring the second man. They had gone over this part.

Scott threw one of the gallon jugs of bleach in the other man's face. Spence had sawed off the top so the man was hit with a full splash of it rather than a modest trickle.

That was the one who screamed.

He rolled on the floor, kicking up dust and clutching at his face. Blood came from his eyes. The flesh that was visible was already pink and scalded. He was screaming so fucking loud. Gun retrieved, Spence ducked back behind the doors. The kid was still screaming.

"Aren't you going to shoot him?" Scott asked, surprised to hear anger in his voice.

Spence shook his head without looking at him. His attention was fixed on what he could see outside. "He'll spook the natives," he said. He drew a bead and fired. Scott heard another scream.

Then it was all drowned out by gunfire. Scott hit the ground and covered his head.

~ ~ ~

Colin stopped in his tracks when he heard the first unmistakable gunshot. A pistol, he could tell, something a little bit bigger than the thirty-two he had given Sunny. He hoped that didn't mean Sunny was lying dead, a smoking hole in the center of his head or behind his ear. Then came the sound of other shots, cascading and covering each other, the way a single drop of rain on a tin roof will lead to a seemingly unending shower of them.

He looked up in stunned disbelief. Of all the ways he had expected this night to go, a shootout had not been one of them. A few discreet bullets in the back of the head, yeah, a quick, tense exchange of fire, sure. But it sounded like there were competing firing squads up there. Everything short of howitzers. Just what the fuck was going on up there?

Colin moved as fast as he could to find out. His knee screamed in protest. His face became a twisted mask of pain, but he didn't care. Pain was temporary; it was in the mind. Colin had to get there. He was probably already too late – the gunfire was half a mile away – but there was always the chance that he could tip the balance one way or the other, or at the very least give some pain to anyone who was foolish enough to still be there when Colin arrived, if Amanda was dead.

But that didn't bear thinking about. If Amanda was dead, then she would just be the last in the long line of things Colin McNamara had fucked up in his life. But it would also be the worst. Colin liked to think of himself as a cynic. But if Amanda died, then something would go out of him for real. Snuffed out like the flame of a weak candle, leaving nothing but smoke and melted wax.

So for the moment, he would leave it at "if." Until he got there, Amanda was neither alive or dead, like that cat his physics teacher had tried to tell him about. If she was alive, he would run to try and help her even if both of his knees were blown off and he was forced to run on stumps. If she was dead, he would teach whoever he found there the meaning of rage.

~ ~ ~

For a moment there was only stunned silence, punctuated by the screams of the man rolling on the ground, clutching at his face as though it were covered in fire ants. Then there was the sound of a gunshot and one of the kids near the front was clutching his chest. He held up his blood-covered hands to the moonlight in disbelief and made a sound like "Oooooooo." It was a sound Karl wished he hadn't heard before.

Then the panic started, and the kids in the front started shooting at the barn. Pike was yelling something, but he couldn't make himself heard. The kids kept shooting; some of them dry firing now, not even knowing it. The dogs ran off, yipping and snarling, startled and resentful from the gunfire. The kids were even more frightened than the dogs were, scared out of their wits by what Karl realized was one man. It was only then that Karl realized just how green most of these people were. Karl smelled piss.

Unable to make himself heard Pike turned angrily away, and saw Karl and the two from the truck standing there next to Sunny and Amanda, who looked as stunned as everyone else. "KILL THEM!" Pike shouted, but it came out muted, looking as though he had mouthed it. The other two got the message, though, and began going for their guns.

Sunny flinched and dropped to his knee. At first Karl thought he might be begging for his life but then he realized that he was trying to get something, most likely a gun he had strapped to his ankle. He admired his foresight, but couldn't help but think he could have planned it better. Amanda never blinked. She never even looked at the men who were about to kill her. She just stared Karl straight in the face, their eyes never breaking contact.

It was funny that she seemed to know what Karl would do before Karl did. Then again, Karl's body knew what Karl would do before his mind quite came around to it.

He pivoted away from Pike, facing the two men, drawing back both hammers on the double barrel. He cocked the slide then pulled the first trigger. The driver of the truck's chest caved in as if someone had swung an invisible sledgehammer into it. He stumbled back, a look of panicked disbelief on his face. He struck the hood of the pickup and stumbled, slumping down, leaving a trail of blood against the bumper. He came to rest in front of one of the headlights, casting everything before him in darkness.

Before the other could react Karl turned, pulled the slide again and shot him. A cloud of the man's blood erupted in front of him. The force of the shot propelled him back. He fell, sending up a cloud of dust where he came to rest.

Karl broke the gun open and dug into his pocket for a new pair of shells. He turned and looked. Most of Pike's men were still focused on the barn and the screaming man, the sounds of the shots behind them having blended to their untrained ears with the sounds of their own undisciplined fire.

But one man had noticed, perhaps goaded on by Pike. He had a pistol. Karl had his shells out, but would not have them loaded in time. He stepped in front of Amanda.

~ ~ ~

There was another shot. Sunny had finally freed his gun, a thirty-two revolver. Sunny pulled the trigger. The recoil sent his arm up in an arc that made Sunny feel as if every tendon in his arm had been jerked by invisible fishhooks. The shot went wide, but it was enough to scare the kid, who in all his fantasizing about gunfights had apparently never imagined that anyone would actually take a shot at him. He shit his pants and threw up his hands. Sunny found he couldn't shoot him.

~ ~ ~

Neither could Karl, though his gun was loaded again. "Throw your weapon at my feet," he said. The kid complied. "Run." The kid did that too. Karl bent down, picked up the gun and handed it to Amanda. Karl did some quick math. Pike had had twelve men. Minus him, the two from the truck, the kid if he was smart enough to run and the two who were lying there bleeding by the door, that left six. Much better than twelve, but still nothing he wanted to take on with two inexperienced people and an unfamiliar weapon with a limited number of shells. If he could just take the head off the snake – He looked up, but Pike had vanished back into the crowd.

He looked at Sunny and jerked his head back. The two men and Amanda moved to crouch behind the truck, the only available cover. "Thanks," Sunny said, panting hard and looking scared – not that Karl could blame him.

Karl shook his head. "Don't mention it. Amanda was right, I should never've been out here in the first place."

"The fact you were saved our lives."

"Well, let's not get ahead of ourselves," Karl said. "We can try and take the truck out of here, but I don't want to give the gang that couldn't shoot straight that big of a target. Might be safer if we just run for the back hills. It'll be dark for another two hours, and with the terrain the way it is they'll never find us."

Amanda shook her head. "We came for Scott. We can't leave without him."

Karl gestured at the barn. "Looks like he's doing better than you are," he said.

"Yeah, but for how long?" Amanda asked. Karl couldn't answer that. "Pike will get them all pointed in the same direction sooner or later, and then they'll be fucked."

"What do you want to do? Charge them?"

"No," she said, a bit defensively. "I just want to take a moment and see what happens next."

~ ~ ~

Pike couldn't believe what had happened. The fact that Scott had been desperate enough to let the hit man loose, he could believe that. The fact that one of the men Bing had brought up had turned against him, he could believe that – though he did wish he could kill Bing again for being that fucking stupid.

The fact that the man had not been blasted to wet chunks of raw meat approximately two seconds after switching teams – That he was having a little trouble processing. That little shit should be dead; instead he had managed to get the drop on three of Pike's men and would have plugged Pike himself if he hadn't turned tail and ran. He, Pike, had to run for safety on his own ranch.

When this was all over he was going to kill that motherfucker's family.

What he flat-out could not believe was that his own men were so sloppy and disorganized that they had not only managed not to obey him, they had managed not to hear him. It was true that he had been using tonight to break in some of the new hands, it was true that without

Bing he had one less person calling for order. But still that was no excuse. That was no fucking excuse.

He grabbed the arm of Finnegan, one of the few men present who was north of thirty, who was staring at the mayhem with a look so dumbfounded Pike nearly wanted to kill him on principle. Pike held up a gun and said, "Get them to stop shooting, or God help me I will." The man's wide eyes got even wider, but he ran for the line of kids who were firing at the barn like they were shooting at a line of invisible tin cans on posts. The barn was as perforated as a coffee can that had had BBs shot at it for a summer. Jets of light flew from the holes that had been made. He waved his arms and shouted inaudibly, looking like an idiot while he did it, but it worked. The kids stopped firing and Pike stepped forward.

"Scott!" he yelled, "Did you survive all that?"

In response there was the retort of the pistols. The shot was low and hit one of the kids in the shin. Pike couldn't help but flinch; he reckoned he could hear the bone break. The kid clutched at his shattered leg and fell to the ground, caterwauling worse than the one by the door. The panic fire started again.

"GOD DAMN IT, STOP THAT!!!" Pike screamed. The kids kept firing. Pike strode over to the one on the ground and shot him in the head. The screaming stopped. So did the shooting. Without even turning to look at the reaction, Pike turned back to the barn. "Scott, I got two people out in this yard who walked into the very lion's den to save your ass. If you don't come out of that barn in ten seconds I'm turning these guns that I've been firing at you on them."

~ ~ ~

Scott froze. He was still on the ground. He looked up at the ruin of the barn wall as if he could see anything.

"Don't listen to him," Spence said. He was still by the door crouched down. Surprisingly few of the shots had been in any danger of hitting him. Most were a foot or two above his head. They had aimed high.

"Can you see them?" Scott asked.

"I can't see past the row of clay pigeons."

"Then how do you know he's lying?" Scott asked.

"Because if those folks did come up looking for you, Pike would have killed them the moment he set eyes on them."

There was the sound of gunfire again. Scott thought he might have heard a scream, then what sounded like return fire, but where the hell would that come from? The gunfire stopped, as if giving Scott a moment to consider. "Could be a bluff," Spence said.

Scott shook his hands, "That's not good enough." He paused. "Besides, he would have rubbed it in my face first."

"Either way, what are you going to do once you get out there? Take them all on? You're not Rambo."

"I don't know, buy them a little time so you can cause more mayhem?"

"I'm not the cavalry," Spence said, "I'm riding this out right here. They start cutting pieces off of you, your screams ain't going to draw me out."

"I don't expect they would," Scott said.

"Then you're going to stay?" Spence asked.

Scott shook his head. "I'm going."

Spence's eyes widened with surprise for half a moment, but that was all the emotion he showed. He just shook his head. "I never took you for a stupid man."

Scott regarded him for a moment. "Neither have I," he said, "But believe it or not, I've done the lone survivor thing, and it's not as fun as you might think. I don't want to take the chance of being the only one to walk away from a place I've led people into again."

He stood up, laced his hands over his head and stepped towards the door. At the threshold lay the man Scott had blinded, who still bucked with the seemingly inexhaustible energy pain had given him, though his voice had grown too hoarse for screaming. He clawed at Scott's boot as Scott stepped over him, and Scott shook him free as gently as he could. But he couldn't come completely free, so he went stumbling into the yard where he would meet his fate.

There was less light than there had been. Someone had shut down the sodium halos, leaving only one headlight to cast the assembled men in eerie silhouettes. There were fewer of those too. Pike's ranks had been thinned considerably – some lay on the ground twitching and moaning, others lay still. The only person he could recognize was Pike. The weak light reflected off his white hair, but his face was in shadow.

"Sunny!" Scott called. There was a moment of silence, and then he heard his call answered.

"Yeah." It came from behind the truck, the one whose headlight lit the proceedings. As Pike's eyes adjusted to the dark he saw that the truck was riddled with bullets. Two of its tires had gone flat and the car lay on a crazy canted angle.

"You alright?" Scott called.

"Considering the circumstances."

"Amanda with you?"

"I'm here!" she called, "Karl too." She said it quickly as if to forestall any more questions. Scott felt a rare sort of pride and gratitude knowing about Karl's decision, though he suspected he had little to do with it. He wouldn't have thought the kid had it in him, and he was happy to be proven wrong. Life, it seemed, was always capable of one more surprise. He wondered where Colin was – had he simply not come out? He was, after all, the mercenary type. Or was there still one more wild card in play that Amanda had just kept him from revealing?

"You guys should get out of here while they still have their guns trained on me," Scott called.

The Pike shape gave a derisive snort. "The time for that has passed. If they weren't smart enough to do that while these boys were ventilating my barn, they ain't going to do it now."

"You're the one who needs to run while he has a chance, Pike," Scott said. "You've got what? Five people left standing with you? There's three armed people standing behind you and a very pissed off killer in front. Do you really think that at least one of us isn't going to make it out? That one of us won't be able to tell everyone what a cocksucker you really are? Cause that all it takes, just one spark to start the fire and then all your little facades will burn and everyone will know you for what you are." He gestured to the bodies on the ground and the barn that was leaking light. "Are you going to be able to make all these bodies and all this evidence disappear into quicklime before someone comes out to investigate? You've been lucky, but this time you've finally gone and over-extended yourself."

"I've gotten out of bigger scrapes than this," Pike snarled. A few of the dogs had returned to the clearing like reinforcements, looking for something to tear into so they could reassert themselves, their eyes shining in the night.

"I don't doubt it," Scott said. "But no one gets lucky all the time. Your only hope is to get space between you and this before the whole shithouse goes up in flames."

Pike raised his gun. "I noticed you left yourself out of the equation."

"That was intentional."

"Awful brave."

Scott shrugged. "Every man has a time. Mine is overdue."

Scott could see Pike tense. This was it, he thought, this was finally it. A gunshot rang out and Scott flinched. He always thought he would meet death with his eyes opened, but at the last moment his body betrayed him. He didn't raise his hands, though.

It didn't matter, because the scream that cut the air was not his.

He opened his eyes to see Pike clutching at his leg. A look of disbelief mixed with rage splayed across his face. He had dropped his weapon, and blood poured down his leg. He turned to see who had dared, and saw a panting Colin walk into the circle, his left leg being jerked along beside him. The bandage on his nose making him look like some crazed science experiment come for revenge.

Pike gasped in astonishment as he clutched the bleeding leg. "Sic 'em," he called.

Scott wasn't sure whether he was talking to the dogs or the men, but only the dogs obeyed. Two mean Dobermans rushed at Colin, who looked near collapse, too exhausted even to raise his gun one more time. The dogs hit him in a full-bodied tackle with the force of a linebacker, so hard that they bowled him to the ground and still overshot their mark, skidding off his battered form some ten yards past Colin.

The dogs righted themselves and started towards Colin again, teeth bared, mouths flecked with foam, when another shot rang out. There was a high yelp as one of the dogs took a bullet in the flank and did a somersault. Sunny had broken cover to save Colin's life. The other dog ran at the sight. Taking advantage of the commotion, Pike turned to what remained of his men. He seemed on the verge of saying something but instead ran into the darkness as quickly as he could.

Colin shouted at him from the ground to stop and feebly lifted his gun, only belatedly factoring in the five remaining armed men who stood in front of him. They could have torn the both of them to pieces in a second, but they didn't. They seemed reluctant. Confused.

The silence was broken by the unmistakable sound of a shotgun being pumped. Karl had walked around the car and now had the five men dead to rights. "Don't make a fucking move," he said, his voice heavy with an authority that Scott had never heard there before. "Or I swear you will regret it." They didn't. "Guns on the floor," he called. They obeyed.

Scott turned towards the barn just in time to see a silhouette detach itself from its side like a bat coming from beneath a bridge. It disappeared into the night, heading in the same direction as Pike. After a moment's hesitation, Scott followed it.

~ ~ ~

Sunny watched as Scott ran off into the night. It was odd that a man who had just seconds before been the center of attention could slip away so unobtrusively, but that seemed to be a gift of Scott's. Sunny didn't know what he had seen, or where he was going, but he could field a pretty good guess. For a moment, Sunny hesitated – did he want to be a part of what was coming next?

The answer soon came: He already was a part. He had been there at the beginning, he would be there at the end. After doing a quick check to make sure everyone's attention was elsewhere, Sunny followed Scott into the night.

~ ~ ~

Pike had done his share of hunting on this ranch. There wasn't much in the way of game, but a few deer made their way down the mountains that bordered it when water was scarce, and on dull days he could always find a coyote that needed shooting.

Now he was being hunted, in his own home. When he got out of this he would take exquisite pleasure in making the fuckers pay. The idea that he wouldn't get out of this never crossed his mind. Scott could make all the smart talk he wanted, but he underestimated just how many wheels Pike greased, how many things he got done. Just how many open hands were held out to him. The truth was this town didn't just want him. It *needed* him, and there was nothing they could do about it. He would be on top again. He'd have to cash in a fair amount of chips to be sure, big chips that he had been holding onto for a long long time. But cash them he would. He would get out of this snare, and when he did ...

"Hello, Pike."

The words stopped him cold. He glanced to his right, turning his head slowly. Spence was standing there, looking like something hell had spat out. He was holding a large butcher knife that Pike recognized as his own.

In clothes, Spence looked lean; out of them he looked positively emaciated. He was clad only in pants, barefoot. His feet were bleeding but he didn't seem to notice. His ribs jutted out, and Pike felt that if he took the time he could number each one. The cuts Pike had carved across his chest arms and belly gleamed vividly in the moonlight. They had clotted now, but had bled a fair while before that, leaving him looking as though someone had painted him in his own blood.

But it was the eyes that well and truly struck fear in Pike's fearless heart. The gleamed in the moonlight, expressionless as marbles. They were the eyes of something that had lain dormant in a cave, never seeing the light of day until it had awoken and come for Pike.

They were eyes that had never known reason, and they were regarding Pike as if he was the only thing in the world.

Pike had one chance. "You're a businessman," he said. "We can work this out."

"I was a contractor," Spence corrected. "But you went ahead and made this a matter of personal pride. Tell me, Pike, are you regretting the last few hours of your life?" Pike began to stumble away. He was wounded, but Spence was shoeless and bled out – Pike had a chance.

Spence leapt forward with a snakelike quickness, and Pike felt the Achilles tendon on his good leg sever. The pain was blinding. He fell to the ground, shrieking. Spence was on top of him. He raised the knife.

"WAIT!" a voice cried out. Pike had never heard such a beautiful word in his life. He was sobbing now, with equal parts fear, pain and relief.

Spence was straddling Pike He didn't set down the knife, he didn't even look at the man who had spoken. "Don't try to stop me," he said.

The voice was closer now, and Pike recognized it as Scott's. "Who said anything about trying to stop you?" Scott asked. He threw something. It landed near Pike's face: a roll of twine rope. Spence looked up, an expression of genuine confusion across his face. Scott was close to them now.

He got down on his haunches so he could look Spence in the eye. "I wouldn't stop you. I just wanted to ask you if you really think that's enough. I mean, how long do you think it took that girl in the video to die? In your professional opinion."

Understanding dawned on Spence's face. Pike began to struggle. Spence hit him hard in the temple with the hilt of the butcher knife. Pike stopped struggling.

"If she survived the roll into the pit – and I think there's a decent chance of that – and wasn't crushed by what Bingham pushed down on her – and I think there's a decent chance of *that* – then it probably took her at least a couple of hours to suffocate. If what Bingham pushed down on her was packed loose, enough it might have taken her a couple of days before dehydration got her."

"A couple of days," Scott said, his voice suddenly sounding very tired. All the exchanges that Spence had had with him had been pretty laconic, but now his voice was filled with a genuine bewildered sorrow. He turned to Pike. "A couple of days buried alive in a hot, stinking pit of trash, all because you thought your son's reputation was worth more than her life." He turned back to Spence, his face exhausted. Up until this point the adrenaline had been carrying him, but now that his life was out of immediate danger for the first time that night, he looked like what he was: a tired man rapidly leaving middle age behind. "Doesn't seem right that this piece of shit should get to shuffle off the mortal coil in a few seconds, now does it?"

"It doesn't," Spence agreed.

"How long can you make it last?" Scott asked.

Spence glanced at the horizon. "Not so long as I would like," he said. "I'm sure we'll have company, and I will have to take some precautions to make sure I am not found. But I can tell you with fair certainty that he will still be alive and regretting his actions when the sun comes up." Scott nodded. "That a problem for you?" Spence called out. Out of the shadows, Sunny Wan emerged. For a moment Scott's face looked as surprised as Pike's had, then he just looked tired again.

Sunny regarded Spence, then looked at the old man struggling beneath him like a beached fish. He was quiet for a moment longer.

"No," he finally said. "That's no problem for me."

"YOU COCKSUCKERS!" Pike screamed, "I'LL KILL YOU! I'LL FUCKING KI-" Spence reached behind him, withdrew his pistol and broke several of Pike's teeth with the butt. Then he bound the old man's wrists and ankles with the rough twine and dragged him back to the copse of trees where the killing would be done. At first Pike screamed out more threats and angry cries, but by the time he reached the trees he was just crying softly. Scott and Sunny regarded the dark place which had consumed the two evil men for a long moment, and then they turned and walked away.

~ ~ ~

The walk back to the barn seemed much longer than the run out into the country had been. They were silent at first, and then Scott spoke. "I would have spared you that," he said.

"Wasn't your choice," said Sunny. Scott nodded. They walked in silence a long while, until Sunny spoke again. "Did we do wrong?" he asked.

Scott considered. "I don't think you can say we did right," he said. "But then again, I don't think you can say we did wrong either. In any case, I don't know what else we could have done. Spence would have taken him one way or the other. He wouldn't have thought twice about killing us to get to him."

"I know he earned what was coming to him, but still ..." Sunny trailed off.

"Yeah. I know," Scott replied.

They reached the yard. Karl still had Pike's remaining men at gunpoint. Scott turned to Karl, Amanda and Colin, who lay flat on his back, panting. "You guys need to leave. I'll give you ten minutes to get to the car, then I'm calling 911 to get some paramedics out here for the wounded.

Karl gestured with the gun to the four sitting men, now with their hands behind their heads. "What about them?"

Scott thought for a moment, then turned to them. Most of them looked young, "You hear what I said?" They nodded, almost in unison. "If I give you a chance to run will you do that? Not do anything foolish that would require us to take a shot at you?" They shook their heads. "Get moving down that road, and I better not see more than your backs." They didn't need to be told twice. Scott turned to Karl. "Give me that gun," he said. Karl hesitated. "Trust me, I'll take care of it," he said. Karl handed it over. "Let's find your shells."

Though the ground had been littered with casings, finding the fat red shotgun shells was easy enough – they looked like the remains of poisonous slugs.

"Make those disappear." Scott said as he handed them to Karl. Karl nodded and slipped them into his pocket. He turned to the others. "You should get moving now. You should all be back in your homes before dawn."

"What about Pike?" Amanda asked.

"We couldn't find him," Scott said. "Sooner you get out of here and I get the authorities in, the better chance they have of getting him."

She looked towards the barn. "And ... the killer?"

"Gone as well," Scott said without blinking an eye. Amanda looked as though she wanted to say more, but Scott stopped her. "We can talk about all of this later, but right now you guys need to get moving. It'll take a while for the authorities to get here, but I'd prefer you have as large of a head start as possible when they do." He turned to Colin. "You'll get them home?"

Colin grunted in the affirmative. He put his arm around Amanda and started to lead her away. Scott and Sunny looked at each other for a long moment, then he followed. Scott watched them go. When they had disappeared from sight, which in the deep predawn darkness didn't take long, he gave a heavy sigh and began to walk towards the barn. The moans of the injured men in the courtyard were unsettling, but he fought against his instincts to call for help right away. They had ended up where they were on their own. He stepped over the boy he had blinded for the second time that night.

The blood on the barn floor was starting to congeal. Scott found a spot that was clean and put the shotgun on the floor. He then took the remaining bottle of bleach and poured it over the stock and barrel. He found a glove, put it on, then picked up the gun, went back outside and threw it in a horse trough. It was much quieter now.

Scott had a cigarette. The edges of the sky were starting to turn pink. He took out his phone and dialed 911.

~ ~ ~

They let Karl off first, dropping him off at his apartment on the edge of town. He hadn't spoken a word since getting in the car, aside from the name of the street he lived on, and looked to leave the same way. As he turned to get out of the back, Amanda reached out and grabbed his arm. He looked down at her, dark rings around his haunted eyes. "Thank you," she said. Karl nodded, then got out and was gone.

Next they drove to Sunny's house. Alicia had waited up for him. She came to the front gate, wrapped in a thick coat to keep off the early-morning chill. Her eyes were red-rimmed and exhausted, but she wore a smile that damn near broke Amanda's heart. Sunny walked to her and put his arms around her. After a long moment he raised his head and then his hand. Amanda and Colin waved back, then drove away.

"Next stop Elmo's Beach?" he asked.

Amanda had her head turned from him, looking out the window. She spoke so softly, softer than Colin had ever heard her speak before, that at first Colin was not sure he was hearing her right. "I was hoping I could go home with you," she said. "I don't feel like being alone right now."

Colin was silent for a few seconds longer than he should have been, but answered, "Sure," as soon as he got over his shock. She turned from the view and looked Colin in the eye, and he could not read what he saw there.

The rest of the drive home went by in a blur. A bone-deep weariness had infected Colin, he felt as though he had been awake for days. The entire night his body had been force-fed great gouts of adrenaline, and he had treated it poorly. Now that it was over and his life was not in immediate danger for the first time since eleven o'clock the night before, he was finally feeling the consequences. He felt like a puppet with his strings cut.

Amanda felt the same way. She stumbled as she got out of the car, her knees weak, and had to prop herself up on the banister on the steps leading up to the porch. She waited for him at the top. He unlocked the door and heard the sound of Zoltan frantically bounding towards the door, a small whine coming from the normally non-vocal dog. He opened the door and bent down to scratch the dog's ears as it pressed up against him with all the force he could muster. Colin gritted his teeth against a cry as the dog nuzzled his bad leg, and managed to stifle it. Amanda walked in past them.

Colin followed to the pantry, took the bag of dog food and filled Zoltan's bowl. He patted the big dog's flank as he dug in, then made his way to the bedroom. Amanda had already made her way in. She had collapsed on the bed, clothes on, limbs sprawled to take up as much space as possible. She was snoring. Colin never met a woman who snored as loud as Amanda. He watched her for a while, a smile coming to his tired face, then limped off to the bathroom, where he took off the bandage on his face, examined the damage to his nose with some dismay, then popped a couple of leftover Vicodin and went back to the bedroom.

He pulled off Amanda's shoes and then climbed in himself, not bothering to get undressed either. She moaned a little in her sleep as the mattress shifted beneath her, but did not wake. Once Colin had settled, she drew closer to him and draped her arm around him. Almost immediately Colin began to drift, but before he did he reflected on how nice it had been to be counted on, and to have come through.

For a moment he felt an odd sense of panic, a kind of reverse déjà vu, as if the present moment were nothing but a well-handled, worn memory that he was already looking back on with regret. He and Amanda would never work together in the long term, and as soon as she awoke he would be cast out of this temporary Eden. He could change, but only so much, and never enough to be who she wanted him to be, let alone who she needed him to be. But then the peace of the moment overwhelmed him. He felt the heat of her body next to his and the light puff of her breath against his neck. The sound of her breathing was like the tide, and it carried him away to a distant shore.

They slept that way, pressed against each other, as peacefully and innocently as they had when they were children.

~ ~ ~

The next time they came together was two days later, on a little ridge that overlooked the landfill. A great steam shovel was digging in the pit seen on Bingham's video, taking piles of refuse with each scoop. It had been at it all morning, and they hadn't found the girl yet.

Scott had brought a six pack up with him, but he and Colin were the only ones drinking, sipping the beer out of their cans as they solemnly watched the machine do its indelicate work.

Russell's wall of stories held a half-page headline that proclaimed "MASSACRE AT PIKE RANCH" in big block letters. The headline had been written by Russell. Sunny and Amanda shared a byline on the story.

When the authorities had arrived, Scott had given them the basics of what had happened: He had discovered a tape of incriminating evidence against Pike, and some of Pike's men had attacked him and brought him to the ranch where he was held against his will until a party unknown attacked Pike and his men, leaving several dead and the rest wounded. He left out the parts involving Sunny, Amanda, Karl and Colin, as well as his presence at the death of Quinn, saying instead that the tape had been brought to his attention by an anonymous source.

None of the wounded men contradicted him. There wasn't all that much to contradict. Scott had been in the barn for most of the night. Most of what he had done had been away from their eyes. A couple had died before the ambulance could arrive, and those who had survived had lawyered up and weren't saying anything.

As for Pike, Scott had no idea where he was. The old man had disappeared without a trace. Scott figured he'd be out of the country by now. There had been some hope of extraditing the son in order to put pressure on the father, but Pike the younger had gone deep underground. His passport had not been used in some time, and the last hotel he had been registered at had not seen him since the events at his father's ranch.

Scott knew that the policemen knew that he was keeping things from them, but there was precious little they could do about it. Among the wounded had been an off-duty cop, and among the dead there had been another one. The SRPD's instinct for self-preservation kicked in, they seemed to realize that if they dug too deeply into any aspect of the case they were likely to draw up dirt on their own.

So they accepted Scott's story, a story that wound up in the Telegraph along with a description of the video that Bingham Earle had made and the identity of the murdered girl. The next day had been kind of awe-inspiring in terms of pure political expediency as Scott watched many of the town fathers and power brokers try and put as much distance between themselves and Pike as possible, all while exhibiting a moral outrage that rivaled the prophets of the Old Testament.

Scott took a sip of his drink and smiled ruefully. He had already sketched out a story with Russell that would draw as many lines as possible to the powerful men who were now scrambling to get far away from the collapsing Pike empire, men who had gone to his house and begged for money, who laughed at his jokes and held their hats in their hands, and now were trying to act as though they had never known the man. It had been a while since Scott had written something he liked as much. He had the bastards dead in his sights. The piece would run in the Sunday paper and feature many color photographs pulled up from the archives. Scott would make sure there was as much collateral damage from this event as he could muster.

A smile creased his face. Sunny gave him a puzzled look. "Just thinking about Sunday," he said. Sunny nodded; he had helped put the article together and shared the byline.

Colin hobbled over to the six-pack and opened up another beer. "What do you think happens next?" he asked. He was using a crutch for his knee but the doctors had told him there would likely be no permanent damage. It would be a long while before he ran again, though.

Sunny gave him a puzzled look. "What do you mean?"

Colin took a sip and smacked his lips when he finished, "Well ..." he said. "Pike has had this place sewn up since the seventies. Now San Rita's open territory on both sides of the law. There's land to exploit, an entire campus of kids who need their drugs. Money to be made. We created a power vacuum and someone, either a hometown boy or someone from outside, is going to try to fill it. There are going to be a lot of power grabs coming up."

"What are you saying?" Scott asked, unable to keep some of the disbelief out of his voice. "Better the devil you know?"

"I wouldn't go that far," Colin said. "Just saying there are going to be consequences to what we did."

They were silent for a few moments more. It was Amanda who broke it. "I wonder how many girls they'll find down there, if they keep digging. It couldn't be the first time that Pike did it." No one could respond. The sunlight began to fade.

~ ~ ~

Amanda checked in at the hospital's front desk and got a visitor's badge. The elevators were out of service, so she ended up walking up four flights of stairs to the long-term care ward. After some trouble she found the room she was looking for.

The room she was in contained only one bed. The lights were off and the shape in the bed was dark and motionless. Amanda approached it tentatively.

There was still a large bandage around the boy's forehead. His face did not look peaceful as she had hoped. Instead his face looked thick and masklike, and somehow brittle, as though it would slide off his skull if touched the wrong way. She drew up a chair and sat by his bedside. He looked young, just a boy, really – just a boy who had come across the wrong man on the wrong night. Not an innocent, she knew, but not this guilty, surely.

She knew that Scott and Sunny were keeping something from her. She didn't begrudge them that. There were some things that could not be told. Scott had a very good poker face, and if it had been him alone she probably would have been left wondering. But whenever she mentioned Pike in Sunny's presence, he got a look that clearly communicated that he did not expect him to be found, and not because he got away. Whenever the killer was mentioned, a look of even greater conflict showed on his face.

Something had happened out there in the night when the two of them had run off, and though she didn't know the details, she felt she could guess at the broad outlines. Evil had consumed evil, and in the aftermath had disappeared.

It was gone, but it had left things in its wake, things that had been forgotten about in the sensation around what had happened at the Pike Ranch – forgotten by everyone but Amanda. It was her job to remember. She always remembered. A price had been paid for what happened at the Pike ranch, and this young man's wholeness had been part of the cost.

So she put her hands together and prayed over him, prayed as she always did that the harshness of this life was truly illusory. Prayed that there would be some mercy in the final reckoning, that he would be in some fashion restored in the fullness of time. Not just for this boy, but for all of them. Amanda had seen things – participated in things, she chastised herself for trying to make her role passive – that she had never thought she would see or do in her life. She felt marked in some way that she would not, or could not, bring herself to, articulate. The fact was, she was in just as much need of restoration as the boy lying beneath her. She was not surprised that tears had come to her eyes.

She sat in the uncomfortable metal chair regarding the boy, until a nurse came and told her visiting hours were over.

~ ~ ~

The next morning Scott sat in Linda's. He was nursing a cup of coffee as he finished up the last of his Tapitio-covered hash browns. Someone sat down in the booth across from him.

He looked up and saw Spence grinning at him. The cuts on his face stood out as dark as pen-drawn lines. "Hello, Scott," he said.

"I was wondering if I would see you again," Scott said gruffly.

Spence's grin seemed to widen. "Don't you mean you were wondering if you *wouldn't* see me? Just hear a rustling behind you some night, and then lights out?"

"The thought had crossed my mind," Scott said. There was no point in lying.

"And that didn't worry you?" Spence asked.

"Not much I can do about it either way."

Spence nodded. "True. The fact is, killing you is *a* solution, but that does not necessarily make it *the* solution."

"Frankly, I thought you'd be smart enough to get out of town."

"I did, for a while," Spence said, "Just came back this morning to tidy up some unfinished business."

"I don't see what's unfinished about it." Scott said. "We've been managing to do a pretty good job forgetting about each other so far." He could not quite keep a note of pleading out of his voice, and he hated himself for it.

"We have," Spence allowed. "I was quite happy with the story your protégés wrote, though I have to say they missed some salient details. Would you like to know about it? What Pike went through before he shuffled off the old mortal coil? I'll give you a hint: It wasn't fun for him." He leaned forward, his grin unseemly. Scott shook his head, and Spence looked disappointed. He leaned back, putting his arm across the top of the booth. "Anyway, the point is that this is just today. I'm afraid I need something more to convince me of my security in the long term."

"And what's that?" Scott asked, suddenly bristling. "If you were going to kill me I'd be dead, so why don't you quit the cat-and-mouse shit and just tell me what's on your mind?"

Spence was momentarily taken aback, but soon regained his equilibrium. "Well, the situation is this: You don't want to spend the rest of your life looking over your shoulder, and I don't want to have to worry about you spilling the beans on me. I need to make sure that you keep your mouth shut."

"What do you suggest?" Scott asked.

"I'm going to offer you one clean-up. Free of charge."

Scott was shocked into silence. Whatever he had been expecting to hear it had not been this. There was a long, stunned moment, which Scott finally broke. "Could I possibly be hearing you right?"

"At a time, place and upon a person of your choosing, I will perform my craft. No questions asked. Think of me as God's own smart bomb, and you get to paint the target."

"You're crazy."

"Sure, that's your reaction now. I would be a little uneasy if you weren't indignant. But just let it seep in. The power over life and death. You know how good I am. You know I won't be caught. At a time of your choosing, you now have the power to erase someone from the face of the

Earth. No one turns that kind of power away. Trust me, I know from experience."

"I won't," Scott said.

For the first time Spence looked frustrated. "Fine, but you don't understand. The important thing is not that you call in the chip, the important thing is that you *have* the chip. The important thing is that while you have said chip, I can rest easy, leaving you and your friends be. And if you do call in the chip, then I will have something on you that will make me rest equally easy. I want you to think hard. There are much worse ways for this to go down."

Scott considered, and when he finally spoke his voice was low. "How would I get in touch with you?" he asked. Spence smiled again. He spoke an email address that he made Scott repeat to him.

"Don't write it down anywhere." Spence admonished, and don't get any cute ideas about trying to track me through there. That's an account built for one-time use. You're the only one who has the address. Until you call for me, you won't see me."

He extended his hand, and Scott couldn't quite shake off the sense of disbelief as he reached forward to shake it. When he did, Spence suddenly gripped it, his smile so wide now that Scott wondered if his face wouldn't split. The skin around his mouth drew so tight that one of his wounds began to bleed.

"I know you don't think you'll ever send a message there," he said. "But one day you will. Mark my words on that one. It'll happen."

With that, he stood up and left the restaurant. Scott pushed his plate away. Somehow he wasn't hungry anymore.

~ ~ ~

Scott couldn't stop himself from shaking as he drove to the paper. He felt dirty, worse than he had felt when he had watched Spence drag Pike away. He drove in a daze, and when he reached the paper he didn't go in. He just sat in the parking lot and lit a cigarette.

It had all started here. Less than a week ago. So much had changed since then.

He looked up and saw Sunny walking across the lot to the building. His protégé. Spence had called him that twice, and for all Scott knew it might even be true. Sunny didn't need his help as a writer or a reporter, he realized now. But maybe Scott could keep him from falling into some of the same traps that he had. Maybe by the time he was Scott's age he wouldn't be so fucking battered by life that he was willing to shake hands with the devil. The last week had rekindled something in Scott, that was true enough. But only partially; there were still parts of Scott that were burnt out and always would be.

He sighed and rubbed the bridge of his nose, closing his eyes. He had been compromised today in a big way, and he knew it. You couldn't make the kind of deal that he just had and then look at yourself in the mirror the same way.

Then again, Sunny, Alicia, Amanda, Karl and Colin were all safe because of the deal he'd made. Wasn't that worth something? Scott was already too far gone to have one more sin make that much of a dent. Maybe that was what he was here for, to take the compromises so the others would not have to. He could carry that weight.

He looked back up at the paper and stubbed out the cigarette. Colin was right. It was a brave new world out there, and someone had to watch the playing field. Scott got out of his car and went to work.

Thank you for reading.
Please review this book. Reviews help others find New
Pulp Press and inspire us to keep providing these
marvelous tales.

If you would like to be put on our email list to receive
updates on new releases, contests, and promotions, please
go to NewPulpPress.com and sign up.

ACKNOWLEDGEMENTS

I'd like to thank my family and friends for their support during the writing of *The Unquiet Dead*. Particularly my three beta readers Neil Fulwood, Matthew Keeley and my brother Devon Wilson, whose input and advice was instrumental in shaping the book.

Equally important was the diligent work of my copy editor Justin Hoeger, whose notes and careful attention were crucial.

Finally my sincere thanks to Shirrel Rhoades and everyone else at New Pulp Press for publishing *The Unquiet Dead* and to you the reader for taking a shot on it, I can honestly say I owe you most of all.

ABOUT THE AUTHOR

Bryce Wilson is a freelance writer living in Austin, TX. He is the author of *Son Of Danse* Macabre: A Personal History Of Horror, a feature writer for Art Decades and Paracinema Magazine and a film columnist for *The San Luis Obispo New Times* for the last ten years. *The Unquiet Dead* is his first novel.

NewPulpPress.com